Seasonal Spectres

CROWVUS

First Published in 2021
Crowvus, Stempster House, Westfield, KW14 7QW
ISBN: 978-1-913182-34-2

For comments and questions about
"Seasonal Spectres"
contact the publisher directly at
the_team@crowvus.com

www.crowvus.com

Contents

Foreword

Susan Crow

A cow is lowing in the byre and a misty shroud covers parts of the red dawn. They call to me to take note: this is the time of year when all bets are off - when the veil between worlds is sheer.

For those with a sense of it, these marvellous stories will sit well with you. They convey a real connection between worlds. They may bring you home with the conviction that there is more to this life than everything you can touch.

Five judges came to the conclusion that the ghostly tales printed here epitomise the belief that "there is something else".

All the entries were read by two judges

who sent twenty through to another two judges. Ten of those were chosen to be published and went to the final judge who chose the three winning entries.

Thanks and respect go to all who took part. It is a wonderful thing to be able to put thoughts into words. Congratulations to John and Simon who produced the three winning stories.

I hope all who sit down with this delightful book will be just a little bit haunted by it!

The Empty Parking Place
John Matthews
1st Place

I stood inches from the bedroom window, dressed in pyjama bottoms, my breath creating a ragged shape on the glass. My eyes weren't focussed on this though, they were drifting beyond the glass window to the endless dark sky, illuminated by millions of stars. How long I had been standing here in the gap in the curtains, I just didn't know, but my chest hairs were desperately trying to trap some warmer air and the feeling in my feet had gone.

In truth, I could have been standing in any room in our house. It didn't matter to me or anyone else, as no one would care…

I had singlehandedly destroyed our family.

Tonight, like most nights recently, sleep wouldn't come easily. So I would stand at our bedroom window gazing at the frosty December sky. I had so many questions swirling around my head which I didn't have the answers to. But staring into the endless night helped me to relax and I somehow felt that I belonged out there. Just floating through the night sky, weightless and free from my torture.

I looked back into the room, 05:30 shone in bright red from my alarm clock by our bed. It had been Christmas Eve when I had come upstairs, it was now well and truly Christmas Day.

My wife, Paula, lay curled up in a tight ball, wrapped up in the duvet on our bed. Only her long, dark hair poked out. I should be lying next to her. Comforting and supporting her but, for now, I was just grateful she was asleep.

I turned back to the window and looked down at our street. Despite the early hour, there were lights on in several of the houses opposite. I imagined excited young children dragging their parents out of bed to see if the big man had been yet. That wasn't going to happen in our house this year though... I had made sure of that.

When I was a kid, this night was so exciting. I could never sleep for more than a couple of hours. Creaks on the staircase, doors squeaking open, and whispered voices. I would lie awake in bed with my eyes glued shut, hardly daring to breathe but desperate to get to sleep. I would be worried that it would never get to Christmas Day. But morning did arrive, and my eyes opened to the delights of this special occasion.

As you get older, the Christmas magic starts to wear thin. First you realise that the big man in the red suit is a fraud. A cruel trick of retailers and your parents. Then a Christmas wish list becomes a what do I need list and exciting gifts are replaced by smellies and clothes.

Finally, when you have your own family, you get to play at being the big red man with weight issues yourself and realise the pressure your parents had to go through.

But the joy of seeing the excitement on young faces is worth every bit of stress.

The smile on my face that had now naturally formed, dropped...

There would be no excitement in our house this year...

Because I had killed Jamie.

I turned back to our bed again, the smell of festive spices from the seasonal tealights dotted around the room hung in the air above Paula, who was still curled up in a tight ball. Two weeks on from the accident, I could still sense the rawness of her pain as she sobbed and howled every night until she fell asleep. The doctor had given her sedatives to help, and I was now worried that she would become addicted to them. Medication wasn't my thing though, despite being unable to sleep myself, so I would spend the small hours wandering through the house trying not to wake Paula up before ending my wanderings in Jamie's room. I would only leave when I could hear Paula's sobs again and I would rush back to our room to console her. But for the first time in our marriage, I could say or do nothing to ease her heartache and pain.

I turned back towards our bedroom window; more lights shone inside the dark houses opposite. The glistening, white road slicing through the middle of the street was lined with parked cars either side of it, their colours stolen with the darkness. But they all displayed sparkling white windscreens and side windows. I traced the two parallel lines of dark cars along the street until it was broken by a gap...

The gap was outside our gate.

I gave up on our window now and walked across our bedroom and out onto the landing. Despite everything that had happened, it was still decorated with gold tinsel and red balloons. Across the landing, past the bathroom, was Jamie's bedroom.

I had been joking and fooling around, as Dads do, when I had driven him home from his final Christmas party.

I walked across the landing and sat on the top step. The darkness was suffocating and never ending, as I tried to make sense of the last fortnight. I was supposed to be head of the family, protecting and raising our family. Instead, I had left it in tatters.

My eyes followed the dark outline of the gold tinsel and red balloons to Jamie's bedroom. His door was pushed back but I could not bring myself to go in tonight. In my mind, I could picture his bed covered in teddies, his soldier fort he got last Christmas in the corner of the room and his huge pirate toy chest at the bottom of his bed. His full Christmas stocking would be draped over it, despite what had happened.

I snapped out of my thoughts...

A noise downstairs...

I was sure I heard something.

There it was again... scratching noises. As if someone was tearing up strips of newspaper.

I went back to check our room out of habit. Nothing. Paula still lay curled up in a ball and I went to say her name, but she looked so peaceful, so I moved back out of our room. I could only make out the top of the stairs again and I glanced towards Jamie's open doorway. No point in looking in there but I drifted in to check anyway. I could make out some dark shapes and his stocking, lying on the pirate chest, but nothing else.

Paula had insisted we still put three stockings up for one last time, instead of two. However, that gesture alone would not change the fact we were now a family of two, not three.

I heard the noise again, definitely not in Jamie's room, and I made for the top step on the landing again. Scratching and tearing sounds were now floating up the stairs followed by human noises. I was sure I could hear a voice. I really should wake Paula, but I guess I had caused her enough problems.

If only I had not made that detour to pick up more Christmas food...

If only I had not been larking around in the car...

If only I hadn't told Jamie I had a better Christmas cd.

Our stairs are in an L-shape, and I slowly made my way down them. The stairs creaked and the red balloons tied to the handrail kept drifting into my path. The faint paper tearing noises were getting louder as I neared the turn in the stairs. Once around this corner, the glass panelled door to the living room would be in full view at the bottom of the stairs.

I got to the corner and stopped; something was not quite right. Light danced up the painted walls by the sitting room door just enough to make out the picture of the three of us on the hallway wall.

Then the smell... It engulfed my nostrils...

Smoke.

The voices and tearing noises from the sitting room were drowned out as fear swept over me.

The house is on fire.

I should have run back upstairs...

I should be looking after my family...

And I should have paid more attention on my journey home two weeks ago.

I quickly made it down the remaining steps, the tinsel on the wooden handrail lifting up temporarily in the draught as I ran to the glass panelled door. Flames were lighting up the room. I could see the mirror above the fireplace, framed with tinsel and the maze of decorations across the ceiling.

I swung open the door...

The heat hit me...

The coal fire was on.

I stepped just inside the doorway and the door closed behind me.

This was crazy. We always let it die down before we go to bed. I couldn't even remember if it was on last night. How the heck was it still on and who had been keeping it fuelled?

But there it was. In front of me; blazing away in the early hours of Christmas morning.

We always had a roaring fire on this day, it was our family tradition. Along with unwrapping our presents together, the smell of our real Christmas tree and a proper turkey dinner to eat.

I looked around the room. The small table lamp was on in the far corner of the room, surrounded by nuts and other festive nibbles. The Christmas tree next to it had its coloured lights switched on, reflecting their miniature beams of light off the red and gold baubles. With all this and the real fire, it was the perfect Christmas scene. As if taken from one of the cards that hung around the room. The leather settee was buried under a mountain of presents, with the curtain behind, slightly pulled back to provide a contrast between the warmth of the room and the white Christmas morning outside.

More ripping sounds...

They were coming from the settee...

Jamie.

Jamie was sat amongst the presents and a pile of shredded wrapping paper

I shouldn't have reached for that cd...

It never made it into the cd player anyway...

The image of Jamie, fear invading his eyes, as the metal frame of my car had closed in on us...

What had I done?

If I took another three steps right now, I would be able to touch him, hold him, and show how much I loved him. But I didn't want to frighten his spirit away, so I crept around the settee and perched on the foot stool by the tree, beneath the window.

Jamie did not look up and he carried on opening his presents. I had to stay quiet, and my muscles started to cramp up as I remained motionless from my viewpoint. I still wanted to stride over to him and take him in my arms. Pull him into my chest and inhale his curly hair. Tell him how much I loved him and never let him go again, but I couldn't.

Jamie wasn't real...

Jamie wasn't really here...

Jamie was a ghost.

I tried to adjust my position on the foot stool to displace the pins and needles which were now running down my legs. If I scared him, he would disappear, and I would lose him forever.

Jamie was dressed in his pyjamas, the blue football ones. They were never off his back. He would only wear something else when they had to be washed. His curly hair hung down over one eye on his pale face and his cheeky smile was gone. In fact, Jamie looked like he was going through the motions. He would unwrap one present then straight onto the next without pausing to look at the gift. He looked like he wanted to get this over with and his face had a haunted look which should not adorn a seven-year-old child.

I mouthed *I love you,* but the words did not break the silence in the room. Only the fire spat and crackled, taking its turn with the ripping of the wrapping paper as Jamie continued to plough his way through the presents.

I had fished the cd out of the door pocket and

managed to open the case with one hand, but couldn't prise the cd from the case with the other. I could not believe I lost control in the three seconds I wasn't looking the right way. Once the grinding noises had stopped. Jamie just sat motionless in the back of the car as if he had fallen asleep. I was unable to reach him, the steering wheel pinning me to my broken seat. Where was my bloody airbag? Our last-minute extras were strewn across the interior of the car. Had one of them hit Jamie on the head knocking him out? Then I heard it. Faintly at first but then the noise was unmistakable. Sirens.

Only a couple of unopened presents remained around Jamie. I had been so fixated on him I hadn't noticed Paula slip into the room, awakened by the commotion no doubt, and she sat silently next to Jamie. Her eyes were red and swollen. She could see him too.

Panic filled my head. Would this push her distraught mind so far away I would never be able to claw it back? She seemed to be holding herself together though, using some inner strength that neither she nor I knew existed. Tiny drops of love twinkled in the firelight as they ran down her face. I had destroyed everything.

The sirens had stopped. Bodies appeared at the side of our vehicle dressed in helmets and protective gear, as they set to work on my wreck of a car. I could see a paramedic frantically searching for a pulse and then grimly shaking his head. The guys in the protective gear now worked frantically to get us out.

The smell of citrus fruit drifted across our sitting room as Jamie rolled his fruit around in front of him. He had opened all his presents and reached the bottom of his stocking. This normally signalled a mass tidy up operation with all the paper being scooped up for the recycling bin, but not this morning.

I looked at Paula but couldn't catch her gaze as she sat fixated with Jamie. I held my breath. Would he go now? Maybe fade away into the glow of the fire and leave us childless forever.

I looked at Paula again, to get her attention, she was in bits now. Her body juddered up and down, as all her emotion leaked out once more. I couldn't resist any longer and eased myself off the footstool to console Paula, but I only succeeded in knocking a bauble from the tree and it bounced along the floor.

"Mum," Jamie said. "It's Dad's bauble."

I gazed down. We all had Christmas baubles with our names on them. Mine was now rolling its way across the floor to Jamie and he picked it up.

It came flooding back...

The paramedics and fire crews had removed Jamie from the car, and I suddenly realised no one was working on me...

I was still trapped. The stupid steering wheel trapping me in.

My eyes darted around. The emergency crews still gathered around the car but with a distinct lack of urgency.

Why weren't they helping me?

They were now putting a blanket over me. I wasn't cold; I just wanted out.

Jamie cuddled into Paula with my bauble grasped tightly in his small hand and she stroked his head.

I noticed my presents weren't out, and I began to lift off the ground, drifting up towards the window. Past the uneaten mince pie and nip of malt whisky.

Paula kissed Jamie's forehead. "Let's tidy up later and we will open Dad's presents one day, when we feel ready."

Jamie just stood there, clutching my bauble.

Paula cuddled him in. "Will you help me with the dinner later on, Jamie?" she said. "Your Dad would still want us to have that."

Jamie nodded and kissed his Mum, before prising himself from her grasp to place my bauble back on the tree. "Love you, Dad."

I mouthed back words of love and I felt a sense of relief as I drifted through the window.

Jamie had been spared. I hadn't killed him. Things would get better for him and Paula. They had all of their lives ahead of them.

I was outside now. The room and my family were gone, and I could just see the dancing flames from the fire as I floated across the garden, out onto the street and through the gap in the parked cars.

Diary of an Unknown Woman:
1862 – 1863
Amanda Jones
1st Place (11 - 16 years)

29th October 1862. Mother always says that if life gets a little rough around the edges, that things always seem to be that little bit easier to figure out if they've all been written down on the page. I have not the first idea whether that is true or not, but I feel as if I am at my wits end, and this is all I can think to do. It's not like I don't like my job – nannying for the darling Edith is simply *wonderful* – but it has all come a little too much. You see, for as long as I can remember, Mother has warned me of 'those charming young men, who'll make your heart flutter. They're the ones who will leave you broken at the altar, the world watching on in your shame'. It is my fault entirely that I have fallen for the terribly chivalrous and awfully kind and torturously sweet widow father of darling Edith. But not once have I felt out of place with Henry and it is because of that, that I fear I have committed a grave mistake. No longer can I look at another man again, for both Henry and I know what we have committed. Society will be cruel, and yet I cannot bring myself to regret it, for every time I look at Henryall I feel is love for him, and love for our illegitimate child. I am sure that the gleam within his eye as he watches back is romance too, and adoration for the family we shall create together.

4th December. It has been quite some time since last I wrote in this, and so Mother must have been right! Thinking back now, I was worried for nothing at all – why I ever questioned Henry's fondness of me is something I will never quite understand. Today's entry is somewhat happier than the last, for it is more me writing as to finally understand that what is to come is true, than a brief bout of nerves, for tomorrow it is to be that I am wed. Marriage. It seems so odd to think that mere months prior I feared for my becoming in society's eyes, and now Henry, kind darling Henry, has commenced such an occasion as to protect my honour. Past Mother's kind words, I do fear she has become suspicious of our relations, but that is of no matter, for we love each other so dearly, and I'm sure she is able to see as much too. The next time I write within these pages I shall be a married woman, and I know that the days to follow will simply be the most perfect of my life.

15th December. It was Edith's birthday today, and yet an air of melancholia seemed to subduethe house. Though Henry promised to take the day from work today for her, he was called away on an emergency appointment earlier this morning and has only just returned this very evening. In no manner am I admitting any sorrow in marrying beloved Henry, but such is the way of being such profound of a doctor, that sometimes work must be put first. Not once has any mention of our honeymoon come up also (Henry pins it on my pregnancy, and surely, he is right).

Today was also the day, five years ago, that Edith's mother died in childbirth.

Though it feels cruel to say so, I am glad Edith does not remember her, for if she had, then her sorrow would be so much more profound, and maybe never would she view me as anything other than replacement to the one she lost. Those words feel foul on my tongue, for how dare I think such a thing, yet it is so true it feels as if it must burst forth from my chest in some dirty admission of my sins.

In attempt to raise the mood of the estate, Edith and I played her favourite games all day long (I never quite realised how much excitement a child has, and I do fear that when my children grow from one to two, I simply will not be able to keep up). Alas, it was the games in which my issue did arise. With the house so large and containing so many secret places, it was Edith's idea to play hide-and-seek. Once one hundred had been counted to, and I went of in search of Edith, it was soon that I did find her, tucked within the corner of the upstairs hallway in tears. Amidst the crying, I was able to make out the reason of her fears. She calls it the room.

We do not speak of the room. It is our well-hidden secret in plain sight. It was only after I enquired to the staff why that singular room was locked, and is key within a drawer, separatefrom all the others, that I finally told in hushed whisper. It is Henry's personal medical room,set up like a hospital in the case that any of whom reside in our home fall ill.

Therefore, it is also the room where Edith's mother passed.

Despite being barred and locked and curtains pulled across its window, poor Edith was certain that, as she passed its door, she saw light within. And within that light, Edith was so adamant to believe, peering out from below the door, shadow, those of feet, pacing before thewood.

Yet when I checked, nothing was amiss. No lights shone out below, the door remained sturdily locked, and the key was still within its locked drawer, dust amassing on its dulled brass. Nothing was amiss, yet Edith, darling Edith, who never told a tale, nor wished to ever stop playing a game, seemed to believe something was wrong.

24th December. I am writing this by dying firelight, and so today's passage will not be long, but Edith is right. It is lucky we had already escorted her to bed, tucked her in and whispered sweet nothings of Christmas and love and gifts galore, for we both saw it. Out of the corner of my eye, creeping out from the hinges of that fateful locked door a hue of yellow shone out. In a macabre sort of manner, it was almost beautiful – memento for life lost, and new hope – but it was also so cruel and so foul that my head spun, and my stomach churned. When finally I broke from my trance, Henry's face was equally as pale as I know mine must have been and, as he pulled me desperately to our own room, I was able to glance back one more.

Light off. Nothing but darkness.

I do not understand how Henry is able to sleep so soundly. I am sure his ashen expression is in response to the same as what I did see. Maybe Henry pretends that all is well as to ease my own mind – he is so dear like that.

11th February 1863. I fear this diary may soon receive more frequent entries. Henry says it is due to my pregnancy that dizziness made me fall today. I can tell he is worried, and I am terrified too, for both myself and for the baby – a trip down a flight of stairs will do that you see. Never have I seen him in quite so much panic as he rushed to collect the key covered in dust from the locked drawer. There was a pain in his expression as he unlocked the hatch, pushing through the stale air (if I think hard enough, I can almost image the remnants of age-old florals lightly touching each surface). The room is not as I imagined. It is simple and plain, with little decoration and nothing to indicate the grandeur of the rest of our home. Henry says the plainness is to rest the mind of thoughts (though personally I fear that it is so boring I shall have to regress to my mind simply to *have* a thought).

It is so that I can be monitored, and the well-being of my baby ensured, that I am to stay in this room until Henry deems me safe. All meals shall be delivered, and all I am to do is focus on myself. Henry jokes I should focus on my balance too, for if I continue to do falls as such, then I will have to stay here until the child is birthed.

(I wish not to tell Henry that I am sure I felt hands *pushing* me down those stairs).

12th February. It has not even been a full day, and yet I am already bored of the room. I can hear Edith outside in the garden, her shrill giggles carrying to my open window, and yet there is nothing I can do but lay on the bed and write. Henry has not brought me anything from our room, and so the vanity in the corner, and the dresser to my side, all lay bare and empty.

Everything is bare and empty in here, and thus it makes me feel bare and empty.

I fear I already I must depart from this moment of solace, for I hear the staff bringing me up my lunch, and if they catch me writing it shall be reported to dearest Henry (he believes that the next few days I should do nothing at all, as to allow my body to focus on repairing itself and 'not writing trivial nonsense').

13th February. The baby has died. I had the most dreadful of cramping, as if my insides were screaming out to escape, and then the blood came. Oh God, the blood. Though I have been wiped clean and dressed in a new nightgown, I can still envision the red coating my legs and my gown and my hands. I don't think I'll ever quite forget that shade of red. Henry will be rushing home as I write, but it is too late. The baby is gone. He promised to protect it – to protect me – and he didn't. ~~I hate him. I hate him. I hate him.~~ No, I must love him. How was he to know?

He promised the baby would be fine.

If only I hadn't fallen, then maybe out perfect family could still come to be.

18th February. I cannot deal with this bed rest for much longer. As soon as Henry leaves for the day and the staff have stopped their pampering, I must get up, simply to walk around this hateful room and see if there is anything – anything at all – of interest.

18th February. I found her diary, Edith's dead mother's. It was slid between the vanity and the wall, a well-hidden secret in plain sight. We seem to have a lot of those. Just simple movement has taken so much energy out from me, and so my reading of the tales within must begin tomorrow, once I have slept.

*****

(Extracts from the diary of Ada Maria: 1858 – 1859)

21st September 1858. I hate the man. He knows I am well and fit to walk, and yet he locks me within this god-awful room as if I am some caged animal. It is a shame I am already pregnant, for things would be so much easier if I were just able to divorce him without a child trying to pull us back together, but alas it is the way the world works. No matter his thoughts that this baby will fix everything he has broken, as soon as I have birthed it, I shall leave this place and everything within. How could my younger self be so enamoured by this man? How could she have pondered our future together during sleepless nights? How could she have not seen straight through his chivalrous smile to the seething animal just behind his skin? I've not long left, just a few months before I can make my escape and never see his false kindness again.

13th December. I feel ready to give birth any second now and I've no idea whether it is my desperation to be rid of this room (rid of this house) or a sign from the child itself. Either way, I am so completely fed-up of pregnancy that if the baby does not appear within the next few days, then there is simply no choice but to tear it from my body myself.

27th December. He calls it the rest cure. For my 'severe nervous symptoms'. I am not insane! Finally, he has admitted to himself that I was never intending to stay, and that is the reason I have been given such a treatment. It is nothing to do with him caring so deeply of me that hewould do anything to have me saved – it is because he is cruel and he is selfish and he is lying and he does not want me to escape! I am to have complete bed rest for as long as it takes for me to be 'cured' (I will never be 'cured' for I never had anything wrong with me in the first place) without any form of mental stimulation nor even the ability to eat my own food. I am to have as much freedom as the baby I have just birthed. Oh, by God do I wish to have the power to do to him that he has done to me. Though I wish I did not care for her, by God do I hope to save my poor sweet Edith from his cruel clutches. He will never love anyone but himself and his sadistic methods of torture in the name of medicine.

24th January 1859. He's putting something in my food, I know it. I feel myself get weaker and weaker, and every time I brush my hair, strands fall out in clumps. I've been brought on a cough too, one that wracks my entire body until I cannot breathe, and I fear I may pass out.

What am I to do though? If he has not already told them I am dead – wept false tears and described the sorrow he felt as I passed in his arms during childbirth – then

I am most certainly seen to be insane. It will only be made worse if I create allegations, for who will believe me?

I fear my only escape now is death. I hope I pass in the morning, when I can watch the sunrise on a new day.

10th February. I've given up. There is no fight left within me. My hand shakes as I write, from the lesions that have spread across my body. It hurts so much, the open wounds on my hands, and the hidden wounds of my heart – of my lost hopes and dreams. I can only hope that someday, I may be able to help somebody else from the same fate as I. Someday, maybe she will be drawn into this room and find this very diary and know the truth. That is all I can now hope for.

*****

19th February. How could Henry have done such a thing? I thought I loved him, but Mother was right all along. My heart feels shattered, and yet I cannot tell a soul the truth, for if he has done something this cruel, then what is the chance he shall do the same to me. What if it is that already he is doing the same to me? What with the miscarriage, there is no reason for him to stay with me any longer. Oh God. If I am to do nothing, then I shall die a scorned woman. I must do something, harm him as he shall harm me, yet my mind is such disarray that I simply cannot think of what to do. I understand that my fate is to die, I am just to hope that it is his fate also.

24th February. I know what I am to do. Though it may not be the safest option to write down my plans between these pages, there is a sort of exhilaration that runs through my body at the prospect of it all being uncovered. It all feels a little surreal – like one of those exciting stories Mother would read me to bed. If only I had just listened to Mother, for all she ever wanted was my safety. I am so sorry lovely Mama, for it is always the ones that you give your heart to too quickly that will take the rest of you apart piece-by-piece.

I am to poison Henry, as he has poisoned us all. Later this night I shall make my way to the cellar and take the rat poison, hiding it beneath this very bed I am laid upon now. After Henry arrives home from work every evening, I shall invite him up to share some tea, and it is then that I shall do to him the very thing that he is trying to do to me.

I must admit though, that I am so concerned for Edith. I simply cannot leave her alone, subject to the cruelty of being an orphaned child. Already she has lost so much, has lost her family of past and of future. The only way I can see the preventing of more suffering, is if I do the same to her as to Henry. At least then, maybe in death we can finally be well again.

18th March. All I can hear is the incessant sound of Edith. She makes my mind spin and forces my focus to be lost. It is often now that I wish that her illness will affect her quicker, so that I can be in peace without the knowledge she is prancing about in those forsaken gardens, whilst I am locked here.

I have grown to despise that child, for the loss she caused to poor Ada, and for every time she comes to visit me, all I can see is the face of that monster Henry. I will be glad when she is gone.

22nd April. I fear Henry and Edith are not ill enough. Though they are bound to their beds for much of the day (by their doctor's orders – how ironic) believed to have a bout of the seasonal flu. It is still not enough. Watching their illness worsen, their eyes sink into their heads and skin paling to almost translucent, skeletons in all but their heartbeats, my own energy has seemed to invigorate. Secretly I know though that somehow Henry must still be poisoning me, but I am gleeful to state that it is unable to pause the joy I now feel. But not enough is happening. They must suffer for what they have caused me, and I am fed up with watching them worsen so slowly.

There is a sort of irony in today. Good Friday: the day meant for celebration of Jesus' ownsacrifice. Surely my own sacrifice of Henry and Edith is celebration above all.

23rd April. I do not know why it is today that has reminded me of months gone past, when still I feared this room, when Edith and I would watch impossible footsteps pace before a locked door. Christmas eve, a day of new beginnings, was the final time I felt unease of this splendid room, for now it has shared its knowledge with me. It was fear that turned Henry's complexion ashen, not of the door, but of himself, a fear brought on by guilt. The room shared to me that it was then he began his torture of me, and now that he has gone, I no longer fear anything. Never once was that man concerned for my well-being – the Henry

I knew and I am ashamed to have loved, was nothing but a façade. This room has saved me, has protected me from the cruel man and his cruel house. It has allowed me to survive, to be reborn, to live another life, just as Ada wished.

His daughter is no better than he, the offspring of a hateful beast and a woman who just wanted to be free. She bears the markings of the devil, hidden within the crease of her smile and the glint of her eye – the features of her father, which make she and him the same. If it had not been for her, then we would have been free, Ada and I, yet both we were trapped, the same moment, five years apart. ~~The girl created this suffering with her mere existence.~~

Darling Edith never knew any different.

*****

The diary slips from her fingers, falling against the hardwood floor with a dull thud. She does not hear it though. She does not hear anything. Not the shrill giggles of darling Edith carrying to the open window, nor her sweet innocent joy as they danced around the house. She closes the curtains, unwilling to gaze outside and see the stillness around her – the absence of life created in her wake. She turns on the light and paces, hands trembling as she reaches toward the door, part of her mind screaming out to open it, to flee, the other begging her to stay inside, to shut out the world and live within blissful ignorance. Creeping out from the hinges of that fateful locked door that hue of yellow shone out, barred only by the shadow of footsteps pacing. In a macabre sort of manner, it was almost beautiful – memento for life lost,and new hope. But the yellow was also foul, and it scented of rotten florals.

The Ghost of the Old Schoolhouse
Taylor Lewis
1st Place (up to 11 years)

I was too sad to cry when Mum told me we were going to move house.

"But all my friends are here Mum!" I shouted.

Mum told me to be quiet and go pack my bedroom up. The next day we went to see the house we would be moving to. It was miles out in the country and there was a huge shed which made Dad very excited. He said it used to be the school but that it had closed fifty years ago.

The shed was actually bigger than the house and Mum said that me and my little sister (who is very annoying) would have to share a room. I asked why Ben (my big brother) had his own room and Dad said it was because he was the only boy.

"And because I am not scared of ghosts," said Ben. "There will be a lot of ghosts here because it is such a spooky old building."

Mum told Ben to be quiet and we went home. One week later we moved in to the old school house.

Everything was very normal to begin with but then one day I saw a strange light in the shed. I thought it must be Dad and I went out to meet him because he must have just come home from work and gone into the old school. When I went into the shed there was no one there and the light had disappeared!

"HELLO?" I shouted. "DAAAAD?"

I was starting to get scared so I ran out of the shed and back into the house. At dinner, I told my family about what I had seen.

"Wooo!" Ben said. "I told you there are ghosts here."

"Be quiet Ben," said Mum.

"I saw a light last night too," said Dad. "I thought it was Ben messing around."

Ben shook his head. He did not want to

get in trouble with Dad.

"It wasn't me," he said.

That night I was very scared when I went to bed. I did not want to look out the window to see if there was a light in the shed. In the morning, I was feeling braver so I went out to have a look.

"Hello," said a voice.

I looked and saw a little girl standing by the window.

"Hello," I said. "Who are you?"

"My name is Victoria," said the girl. She was wearing an old-fashioned dress and had curly hair. I thought she looked like someone in a book.

"Do you live near here?" I asked.

"Yes," Victoria said sadly. "I live here."

"Here! But this is our shed!"

"It was my school first," Victoria said. "I was the last pupil here one hundred years ago."

"You are a ghost!" I exclaimed.

Victoria nodded. "Yes I am a ghost. When all my friends went out at the end of term I got left behind and the school closed so I was all on my own."

I had thought that if I ever saw a ghost in real life I would scream but I just felt very sad when I heard Victoria saying what had happened. I missed my own friends but at least I could still ring them or Skype with them!

"Will you be my friend?" Victoria asked me.

"Yes of course," I said. "Come on! We can go play!"

When I told Mum and Dad about my new friend Victoria the Ghost, Mum said that I would get some real friends when school started and Dad said he had a pretend friend when he was little so maybe I got it from him. I did not care that they thought Victoria was pretend. She was my friend and I was her first friend in one hundred years!

One week later an old lady came to the house to bring us a NEW HOME card.

"It is nice that this house is being lived in again," she said. "No one wanted to buy it when they heard the story."

"What story?" asked Dad.

"One hundred years ago there was a big fire in the school. All the children got out apart from one little girl who died."

"That is very sad," said Mum.

"Yes," said the old woman. "After that, everyone said that there was a ghost in the old school so no one wanted to live here. Actually the ghost was my aunt. Her name was Victoria."

42

Grandmother's Footsteps
Ellen Evers

The Mini halts in a spray of icy gravel and I scramble out, promising to text a time for pick up. Alex wants to come too but I feel that this is something I have to do alone. As the car skids off, I take a moment to look with fresh eyes at Rathbone Hall, covered in an icing of snow, the place I've called home for most of my twenty-five years. Its shabbiness is not endearing; I'm not interested one jot in its historical past. To me, it is a white elephant and the quicker I can get rid of it the better.

I half run to the back door, slipping and sliding, cursing my lack of suitable footwear and fumbling for my key. The phone call from Martha this morning came as a shock.

I'd only seen Gran a couple of weeks ago, maybe a month, and she'd been fine then, hadn't she? I struggle to remember. My visits were, I admit, short and sweet, but the saintly Martha would have said something, wouldn't she? I would be visiting tomorrow as it was Christmas Day anyway, but this seems like an emergency. I let myself in and run up the back stairs to Gran's apartment, calling out as I go.

Martha appears immediately. She looks even smaller than normal: she seems to have shrunk, looking weary and dowdy in her habitual black.

"How is she?" I ask breathlessly as I'm beckoned into the sitting room. I'm alarmed to find Gran is not in her usual chair overlooking the parkland.

"Doctor's given her a sedative - she's drifting in and out. She's fighting it – wants to see you and won't rest 'til she does."

Martha, my Gran's lifelong companion, looks at me with her usual Scottish Presbyterian disapproval. Gran might love the bones of me, but Martha knows me too well.

Wordlessly, she leads me into Gran's bedroom, ill-lit and fuggy with no windows open. The figure in the bed doesn't look like Gran: she too looks smaller, childlike almost. Her mouth is open slightly and she breathes gentle snores.

Gran.

She's been both mother and father to me when I'd been orphaned so young. I love her: sure, I do, but I don't want this life. I've shied away from actually telling her, she must have guessed but refused to face it. I have other plans and they don't involve this decrepit heap.

As soon as I approach the bed, her eyes open.

"Caroline, thank goodness you're here." She struggles to sit up. I grasp her hand, holding it tightly.

"Shush, Gran, it's okay."

She becomes more agitated and then begins to cry, soft snuffly sobs.

"I've seen her Caroline, I've seen her!"

I glance at Martha and raise my eyebrows. Surely dementia doesn't come on this quickly?

"I need to talk to you Caro, I need to tell you. It's time, I know, because I've seen her!" She turns her head to Martha, dropping her voice. "It's not a glimpse this time, I've really seen her."

Martha comes close and wipes away the old lady's tears carefully with a tissue.

"You have a little sleep, dear. I'll talk to Caroline and when you wake up you can have a wee chat." Her voice is soothing and I can see Gran's calming down.

We leave her and return to the sitting room. Martha disappears into the kitchen and returns with a tray laid for coffee.

"Who's she supposed to have seen?" I ask as Martha pours and passes me a cup.

She doesn't speak for what seems a long time.

"This is going to sound very far-fetched, and I'll understand if you think it's a lot of nonsense."

I shrug. "Who's she seen?" I persist. She continues to sip her drink.

"The French Mistress."

I laugh then, I really do. Gran's worse than I thought. She must be really losing it.

"That's just a daft story for the punters to spice up the boring tours a bit. It's not true, it's just a story." I thought Martha had more sense.

In my school holidays I'd done some of the guided tours in the Hall, under sufferance I might add. This French Mistress story went back to the first Earl of Rathbone, seventeenth century I think, in a time when the family had money. According to legend, he kept her prisoner in the attics, where she could be heard walking up and down in the exquisitely embroidered slippers she loved.

One Christmas, an especially bad weathered one, she mysteriously disappeared. Died in the snow perhaps. Nobody knew until the skeleton was found years later. The ghost supposedly haunts the Hall, appearing on Christmas Eve. The sound of her footsteps can be heard in the depths of the night, as a precursor to the apparition's appearance. Absolute nonsense of course but visitors, few and far between unfortunately, love a ghost story. That was the best part of the tour as I remember, and I relished telling it.

"So, Gran says she's seen the French Mistress. Come on Martha, you can't believe that surely?"

Martha finishes her coffee.

"Don't mock that which you do not understand," she says with quiet determination. "And there is more that you must be told. Your grandmother will speak to you, but I will prepare you first."

She stands up and walks to the window. I wonder if they'd both gone loopy at the same time. This is too weird for me. I need to get out, but Martha was not to be rushed.

"Part of the legend remains a secret within the family. It is said that the Earl's *grandmother* helped him to dispose of the mistress he'd murdered. So, the curse was put on her."

She wraps her arms around herself as if chilled by her tale.

Curse? First I'd heard of a curse. That would have brought the punters in, I think irreverently, trying to keep this light and failing.

"The French Mistress must have been afraid for her life. It wasn't until sometime after, not sure how long, that a letter was found in the attic which decreed that unless her slippers were secretly guarded and kept safe in the Hall by each grandmother of the generation, destruction would come to the family and the Hall."

It is my turn to shiver now. This is getting crazier by the minute.

"They didn't believe any of this at first and the first thing the grandmother and the lord did was to get rid of the shoes. They sold them as soon as they could for little money. They just wanted them gone." She pauses for effect. "The lord died of a stroke before the end of the day. His grandmother bought the shoes back."

I have no idea how to respond to this so

say nothing.

"Do you remember the fire that destroyed the West Wing at the turn of the last century?"

I nod. I have a faint memory of the chapter in the guidebook.

"The Lord Rathbone of the time didn't believe in the curse and refused to entertain such nonsense. He regretted trying to get rid of the shoes when he saw what damage had been done. So, after that, they have been protected, just as the French Mistress demanded."

I can't help it. I think what I've planned for Rathbone Hall. The shoes will fetch a pretty penny on eBay, curse or no curse. There won't be any Hall left here to protect them.

"So, through the years, the task of keeping the shoes safe and secret has rested with the grandmother...and granddaughter." Martha pauses and looks directly at me. It is my turn to stand and pace.

"The legend says that the Christmas when the grandmother sees the apparition it is time for her to pass on... the responsibility to her granddaughter."

A cry comes from the bedroom and we both rush in to see what's wrong. Gran is struggling to climb out of bed and, with difficulty, we manage to settle her. Her eyes are restless, but she seems a little more coherent.

"Have you told her?" she rasps, grabbing my hand. Martha nods. Gran squeezes harder.

"Listen to me Caroline. When I was your age, my grandmother told me the story and I didn't want to believe it either, but I've done my duty and now it's your turn." She puts out her hand and gently strokes my hair.

"Promise me you'll keep the shoes safe here in Rathbone Hall until you pass the estate on to your granddaughter. Only then will our family survive."

Granddaughter? That's a joke. I wondered what Alex would make of that. Not exactly part of our life plan. Martha looks at me and then drops her gaze.

Gran gestures to Martha, who crosses the room and carefully takes down a picture behind which is a large old-fashioned wall safe. She turns the dial several times; the door opens, and she pulls out a dark brown casket. Carefully she carries it over and lays it on the bed. With shaky hands, Gran opens the lid and removes a bundle of cloth which she unfolds to reveal a pair of strange looking shoes. They're tiny enough to fit a child, made of thick faded pink brocade that may have once been red. There's a stale, musty smell – distinctly unpleasant.

"I have not seen these in fifty years," she whispers, staring at them, transfixed. "I wanted to put them from my mind... but, when I saw her, I knew it was time."

With trembling hands and a fearful glance at Martha, she wraps the shoes up in the cloth. I'm glad to see them covered and returned to the safe: they give me the creeps.

Gran seems to relax a little and takes my hand.

"Thanks, darling girl," she whispers, closing her eyes, and we creep out.

Once back in the sitting room, I ask, 'Have *you* seen her?'

Martha shakes her head.

"Only the ones who carry the burden have seen her fully at the proper Christmas time, although sometimes they may catch the briefest glimpse..." She looks up at the ceiling. "I've heard her though, walking up and down the attics in the last few days. I think your Gran has too, but we don't talk about it." She sits wearily, as if energy has drained from her.

"Martha, all this about me taking on this

'burden' as you call it, you know it won't work. This place is a money pit. I won't have the cash to keep it going when it passes to me. It's losing money hand over fist."

She looks at me anxiously. "What about the National Trust?"

Donate my legacy to the State? I don't think so. My silence speaks volumes.

This is not the time to confess that Bellport Homes will be building a lovely modern estate on these grounds, called Rathbone Hall, which I think is a classy touch. I'll even make sure Martha has her own house because this place will be coming down brick by brick. The developers are very understanding and know they have to wait for nature to take its course, but it's only a matter of time.

Sorry, French Mistress, your reign of terror is over.

It's time to leave and tell Alex this bizarre tale.

"Got to go," I say, furiously texting. "Alex is picking me up." Martha's mouth tightens. I spend a few minutes with Gran, who seems better, then I hear the Mini's toot.

Making my farewells and promising a visit tomorrow, I escape and skitter to the car.

Something makes me look back and I swear there's a shadowy figure standing at the attic window. This is really spooking me, I think with a shiver, clambering into the front seat.

"Is she okay?" asks Alex, leaning over to brush her lips with mine.

I sigh.

What would my partner make of all this? I take her hand and squeeze it.

"You are so not going to believe this...let me tell you a story. About some shoes...and a Christmas Curse."

My voice is light and jokey, but I feel a dread that I can't shake off.

She listens without interruption at my scathing report of old ladies who have lost their wits and how gullible people are. And my eBay plans.

I don't mention the figure that I'm sure is still watching over us.

"Well, say something," I snap, as Alex gazes through the windscreen, which is thickening with snow by the second. I'm freezing and just want to get the hell out of there. But my partner doesn't move.

"What if it is all true? Think about it for a minute. What if you do demolish the Hall when it passes to you? You've destroyed your whole family history, not to mention the shoes. Doesn't that scare you?"

She turns to me, serious as sometimes she can be.

"Caro, why not think it over?"

"Can't see us getting a granddaughter though, can you?" I smile, although my eyes flit to the window above.

Alex shakes her head. "Nothing's impossible today, is it?"

She's right.

I imagine Gran's face as I take on the burden and save the family. The thought of a child of our own fills me with wonder, and as for a granddaughter...

I look up at the attic window. The tall figure has gone.

The Black Kist
Alistair Chisholm

Now, off away from the road to Glenshee, up in the low highlands, the world gets pretty thin. You might pass a mile or two between houses, and the villages are only a few cottages and perhaps a post office. It's a quiet place, a working farm place, a place where folk are on their own for much of their time. The younger ones often leave, to Edinburgh or Glasgow or beyond, and those that do rarely return. But Fraser Reid returned, and he brought himself an English wife, and they took over the old MacAlpin house on the hillside.

Fraser Reid was an artist, you see. He painted landscapes and sold them to the city galleries. Nothing too challenging –

traditional scenes for customers who wanted calm and things they understood. After the war there was a market for this, a kind of nostalgia, perhaps. So he returned for the scenery, for the countryside of Perthshire was everything he and his clients wanted – craggy but beautiful, wild but not too wild. And his wife followed, as dutiful wives did in those days.

Not that Lilian Reid was overly dutiful. In fact, she was something of a shock to the locals – a strong-minded, self-willed, and very modern woman, with a sharp Lancashire wit and a habit of looking men straight in the face. She had a lean body and muscular shoulders – mannish, some said. She'd been a Land Girl: she'd worked motor repair during the war, and she felt she'd measured her worth. She came with Fraser because she loved him and because, as a sculptor, she didn't mind where they were, so long as she had clay and good light and space.

And they settled in, and converted one room to a studio, and they lived very happily.

There were no children, and the local wives clucked in sympathy, but Lilian wasn't troubled. She knew fine that Fraser longed for a son, and she didn't mind the idea herself, but she was in no hurry. A discreet visit to the Marie Stopes clinic in the city, and some careful watching of the calendar, saw to that for now. The wives clucked, too, for Lilian's other lacks. She wasn't much of a cook, feeding her husband tinned spam and hard-boiled potatoes. She dressed in clay-spattered dungarees, even when picking up her groceries in the village. And the story went that Fraser often had to darn his own socks and jumpers; either that, or Lilian's sewing hand was as crabbit as her stirring one.

But they seemed happy. They worked together in the studio, when Fraser wasn't away selling his pieces, and they always seemed to have a shared joke and a smile. And so folk shrugged and life went on.

Until, that is, the black kist arrived.

Lilian was in her studio when it came. The delivery men raised their eyebrows at her clay-thick fingers and clothes, and asked pointed questions about the man o' the house, but Lilian just smiled. The men heaved in a crate and left, shaking their heads.

Inside the crate was a wooden chest. It was squat, almost square, of thick old oak, roughly jointed. There was an iron handle on each end, and a heavy lid on iron hinges, held closed by a clasp.

It was an ugly thing. The angles weren't even, and the ratio was wrong, somehow, and its oak sides were gnarled and pitted and stained with a curious black tarnish like charcoal. The insides were black as well, and unfinished, plain old rough wood. It smelled faintly of camphor, and something sweet.

There was a small card inside. It read, *To my darling Fraser, and his wife. Love, Edith.*

At this, Lilian Reid's mouth pursed, and her eyes darkened.

Edith McNab had been Fraser's aunt. In fact, she wasn't really his aunt, but a friend of his mother's who had known him since he was a bairn. She'd died in the spring, still relatively young, from tuberculosis, which was common enough in those days. Lilian and Fraser had returned early from their holidays to attend the funeral: Fraser, because he had always been fond of her; and Lilian, to be sure "the old hag is really dead."

For Lilian and Edith had never quite got on. Edith was clear that Lilian wasn't good enough for 'her Fraser', and all Lilian ever received from her were flint smiles and barbed comments. Edith didn't approve of Lilian's homemaking skills. She didn't approve of Lilian's lack of deference to Fraser, or her reluctance to cook, or her sculptures ("nasty, suggestive lumps"), or the way Lilian felt her own artistic endeavours were as important as her husband's.

It made for frosty visits. Fraser was embarrassed – he couldn't understand Lilian's anger. "Och, you know how it is," he would mutter, placatingly. "She's just looking after her nephew."

But that was another point – for Lilian suspected that Edith's interest in Fraser wasn't entirely proper. When they visited, she would lavish attention on him, press him to accept cakes and glasses of sherry, ask how 'my young artist' was getting on. She would pat the seat next to her for him to sit, and lean in closer than Lilian thought necessary, and wear strong, sticky-sweet perfume that wafted in clouds. Occasionally, as she talked, one hand would fall casually onto Fraser's knee, and stay there.

Well. She was dead now. And, if Lilian occasionally smiled at the thought, then we are none of us angels. The woman had left Fraser some money, which they'd used to refurbish the studio.

And now, it appeared, she had also left them this chest.

"It's not a chest," said Fraser, returning from a gallery trip that evening. "It's a kist."

A kist, in Scotland, is a wooden box, sometimes for money, mostly for blankets, to keep the moths out. It's usually plain and unpretentious, as if decoration would be sinful for such a basic function. One above and one below, some folk say; for a kist is also a word for a coffin, and *kisting* is the act of placing a body into the earth...

"A kist, then," said Lilian, irritably. She didn't like it. And she didn't like how Fraser gazed at it, as if at a precious gift.

"It's a family heirloom," he explained. "The *Kist Dubh*, it's called – the Black Kist. It's very old, six hundred years at least. They say Bonnie Prince Charlie hid in it one time."

Lilian looked pointedly at the inside, too small for a grown man. Fraser shrugged.

"It's just a story." He smiled. "I mind as a kid, hiding in it. It used to sit at the end of her bed."

"It's not sitting at the end of *our* bed," muttered Lilian.

#

Autumn died early that year, and by October the weather was hard and black. Fraser had painted through the summer, while the light lasted, and now was the time for selling, so each week he piled his pieces into their ancient Hillman Minx and set off to Glasgow or Edinburgh to visit the galleries.

Those were long days. The rain didn't bother Lilian, or the darkling light, but the cold made the clay hard to work, and the silence of the hillside was ominous. When Fraser returned, he was often tired, and sometimes dispirited.

But they were young, and there were more good days than bad. One week he sold eight landscapes to three different galleries, and they were, for a moment, *rich*. Lilian cooked steaks and Fraser brought back a bottle of champagne, and they toasted their fortunes until they fell over each other, giggling, as they stumbled up the stairs and made shivering love under the cold sheets.

It was the thin hours of that morning when Lilian crept to their tiny bathroom in the dark, to pee, and remove the clever little device from Marie Stopes, and hide it at the back of the cupboard. The moon was up, pale and ghostly, and the house creaked in the wind.

"Aye and keeping secrets, is it?" said a voice.

Lilian spun in shock. No one was there,

but she was sure she'd heard it. A sharp, scornful, knowing voice, just behind her, as if hanging in the air. Now, Lilian was a level-headed woman, and not one to cry for help at sounds in the dark. Instead, she reached for the doorhandle, turned it slowly and quietly, and swung the door wide open in one movement.

Nothing. Her imagination, she thought, and too much champagne. Nothing but the empty landing, and the darkness from downstairs, and the moonlight catching puffs of dust.

"Keeps her house like a pigsty."

"Who's there?" snapped Lilian. But there wasn't anything. Except, perhaps, a faint stirring on the stairs, a shift of shadows... She picked up the torch they kept on the landing and crept downstairs. Into the living room, and still nothing. She took a step, another, another—

And *crack!* – she smacked her shin right against the edge of the kist! Collapsing, Lilian dropped the torch and heard it smash against the ground. She reached out to catch herself and a splinter from the wooden lid drove deep into her hand, and she screamed...

Fraser awoke to the sounds of crashing and swearing, and staggered downstairs to find his wife sprawled on the ground, holding her shin, holding her bloody hand, torch glass on the floor, and a dark red stain on top of the kist.

"Good God, woman, what happened?" he shouted.

And Lilian would have shouted back... But just then, a curious lethargy swayed over her. She felt suddenly exhausted, and weak as a child. When Fraser lifted her up, she didn't protest. When he led her to the kitchen to wash the wound, she stood meekly and let him.

The kitchen light was bright, and the room full of the sound of rushing water, and the hiss of the kettle on the stove as he made her tea.

And, behind her, she thought she heard laughter.

#

In the morning, Fraser stayed home at first. He made Lilian show him the cut, swollen and angry, and insisted on treating it with iodine. He watched her as if she were an invalid. Lilian, embarrassed, grew snappy, and they rowed. Eventually Fraser left, with a sullen expression on his face and his mouth chewing on words he knew better than to say out loud.

Lilian watched him drive off, feeling hot

and angry with herself. She checked her hand again. The cut was long, but not deep. It itched. The top of the kist was stained with the dark red smear of her blood.

She tried to finish the sculpture she was working on, but her palm stung, and the clay felt heavy and stupid, and the studio was too cold, and the shifting light outside made her eyes hurt.

"And is that any way to treat your husband?" asked a voice.

Lilian whirled and stared. Through the studio doorway, she could see into the living room, and the black, malignant, squatting chest. She stabbed a finger at it.

"Shut up!"

For she knew that voice, oh, she did. She knew its scratching, sly tone, and how it could turn on a note into a simpering flirt. And the studio smelt of cold clay and kerosene, but something else, too – sticky, sweet perfume...

"At least I make an effort, dearie."

Lilian Reid strode into the living room, grasped the wooden box by one handle and heaved it into the far corner, out of sight of the doorway, and threw a blanket over it. She returned to her studio, shut the door, turned the wireless up to full volume, and got back to her work.

She finished the piece, though she hated it.

"What's that supposed to be? Who would pay good coin for that?"

She started another, and hurled a slab of perfectly fine clay out into the yard in frustration.

"He came to visit me, you know. On his own..."

She cleaned the kitchen in a whirl of efficient fury.

"A man who's not satisfied at home will aye look elsewhere. It's only natural..."

By the time Fraser returned that evening, Lilian's eyes were dark with fury, her mouth pressed like iron. He was cheerful; two of his pieces had sold! Lilian said nothing. *And he'd met a new gallery owner on Buchanan street, and had a new commission!*

"And did you show them any of mine?" she asked.

At this, Fraser's cheerfulness wilted, and he became wary. Shifty, more like. For the truth was, he had not. The truth was, Fraser was rather embarrassed by the wild, forceful, and anatomical pieces his wife created. He found it hard to show them to the gallery men (for it was always men, of course).

He hesitated too long, and Lilian erupted. *Why* had he not shown them? Why, when he was the one able to go out, and she was stuck here? When the gallery owners would only talk to men? Why? Was he scared she might be more successful? Would he rather keep her here like a *pet*?

Fraser, at first guilty, quickly became defensive and then angry. He pointed out that he had given Lilian a lot of leeway as his wife. Did he complain when dinner wasn't on the table, or his shirts weren't ironed, or that she apparently could not find the duster? He did not. Why, he was even happy to pay for her clay! And was this the gratitude he received?

This fared about as well as you might imagine, and when Fraser went to the living room to get a drink, Lilian followed, snarling with fury. She noticed the room seemed dark, as if smoke had backed up from the chimney. It gathered in the corners, and under its blanket, the kist seemed to shiver...

And in a moment, all the force left her. Her anger dissolved, and she became dizzy. Her last thought was that the smoke was forming a shape, like a smiling mouth... And then black.

#

She dreamt, and in her dream, she was in a box. Its wooden sides pressed against her as she knelt, curled up like a mouse. The lid pushed down on her head, the wooden base was sore and hard against her knees, and her hair hung about her face. Her muscles burned but there was no way to move, and the air was meagre and smelled of camphor, and charcoal, and a sticky sweet perfume...

When she awoke, she was in her bed, and Doctor Lorne was there. He seemed cheerful, but behind him stood Fraser with a worried expression.

Doctor Lorne explained that Lilian was suffering from nervous exhaustion and hysteria. He insisted she stay in bed and rest. He explained it to Fraser, as if discussing a child. When he turned to Lilian, he patted her hand.

"Rest, and calm," he said jovially. "You've been overdoing it, lassie! Heaving all that clay about, eh? Take it easy, there's a good girl."

Lilian, heavy as lead, found herself unable to argue. For two days she slept, or lay hardly awake, listening to the wind and rain, and the creaking house. Occasionally, she thought she heard Fraser talking to himself. Once, she thought she heard someone answer.

On the third day, she dragged herself up and sent her husband away. She was fine, she assured him. The galleries were waiting. He should go. Fraser protested, but Lilian insisted, and eventually he agreed, and, with a mixture of guilt and eagerness, he loaded up the car and set off. Lilian waved from the doorway and didn't let herself sag until he was quite out of sight.

That day, she tried to assure herself that the house was still hers. It seemed fine. The black kist was there in the corner, under the blanket, but she ignored it. She did a small amount of mending, ate a light supper. She slept a proper sleep and awoke feeling better.

The snow started that morning, and she watched it from her kitchen. Huge, heavy flakes fell like blankets and the glen disappeared into white. She felt her world shrinking. Fraser was embarrassed by her. Doctor Lorne patted her hand like a child. She watched the snow fall, in a daze.

"Too proud to lift a finger, that one." said the voice, and Lilian awoke and snarled.

"Edith!" she spat. "Edith McNab I know it's you!"

She knew it like she knew herself. Edith McNab was in her house, *her house*. She stormed back into the living room, and there it was, the black smoke, the shapes, and the smell...

"He couldn't wait to get away, eh?"

"Shut up!"

"A woman should honour her husband..."

She ripped the blanket away and flung open the lid of the kist. There was nothing. Just the plain wood as before, with the strange burnt black insides. Nothing. "I know you're here!" she roared. "Show yourself!"

The telephone rang.

Lilian stared at it in shock, then answered it. It was Fraser, and she sagged with relief.

When would he be home? she asked. But the news wasn't good. The roads were blocked for the snow, he said. He was in a hotel further down the glen. She heard the chink of glasses and conversation in the background.

Lilian tried to hide her disappointment. Of course, that couldn't be helped. Of course, she was fine. Of course...

From the bar came a woman's voice, a young woman. And now Fraser said he had to go, that was the pips, he would see her tomorrow—

The line went dead. Around her, the

black smoke curled, and laughed.

Lilian set the phone down, carefully. She stepped outside, into the snow, and returned with red murder in her eyes, and the wood axe in her hands. The black smoke was everywhere now. A shape lurked near the kist. The smell of perfume made her want to gag.

She took one deep breath, raised the axe, and smashed it against the lid of the kist.

Splinters flew and ricocheted against the walls. She raised it again, smashed it down again.

The air frothed. She raised it again...

And the smoke *inhaled*, and all the force in Lilian's arms disappeared. The axe fell from her numb fingers, landing behind her with a crash. All her will seemed to vanish, absorbed into the smoke. And in return, the smoke shimmered and solidified into the shape of a woman.

As Lilian watched in shock, the figure of Edith McNab stretched, cricked its neck, and sighed.

"That's better."

It gazed at Lilian. Lilian tried to speak, but her tongue wouldn't move.

"You're no what he wants," it said. *"Look at you, wi' your modern ideas, and your*

man's clothes, and thinking you're aye so clever..." It shook its head. *"A man expects respect from his wife. A clean home. Dinner on the table. Well..."*

It lifted one hand, and to Lilian's horror, her arms jerked upwards. It smiled.

"Let's make this place fit for a husband, shall we?"

It stepped away, and Lilian, helpless, followed it.

Lilian worked, and the thing laughed. Like a puppeteer, it controlled her as she tidied, dusted, and mopped each room. It made her cut vegetables for soup, and bake fresh bread, kneading the dough until her arms ached. It led her into the studio, and, helpless, she cleared everything from her half, throwing it out, piece by piece, until there was nothing left of hers.

Inside her head, she wanted to scream, but couldn't. She hardly even knew what she thought.

All her will was someone else's.

"And the kist, dearie," said Edith McNab.

Powerless, Lilian bent, took the handle of the black chest, and dragged it towards the stairs. She heaved it, step by step, up to the landing, then into the bedroom, and sat it at the end of their bed. The creature followed her.

"That's better. Now..."

It tipped its head to one side, examining her. Then it changed, to a younger, taller woman.

The hair turned brown, the eyes flicked blue, until Lilian was looking at herself.

"There," it said. "What do you think?"

Lilian stared back, aghast. What did she think? She couldn't think at all.

"Ah, but we can do better," this other Lilian said. "Can't we, dearie? If we make an effort?"

And now the eyes, so shrewd, softened. The mouth untwisted, the lips became more red.

The waist narrowed, the hips widened; the bust grew larger and the strong shoulders thinned.

"You see?" it said, almost kindly. "You were *never* what he wanted. Not really. But I'll treat him right. I'll give him what he wants." It reached up and rested one hand on its belly. "Everything he wants."

It smiled. "Dinnae worry, though, we'll still let you stay. For the housework!" The red lips curled. "But a woman should ken her place."

It reached down and opened the lid of the

kist.

"In you pop, dearie."

Lilian stared into the chest. Her limbs trembled. She lifted one foot and stepped inside. Then the other foot. Then she knelt. The wood was hard against her knees. The sides trapped her. She tried to find her will, but it was lost to her. She reached, but it was like grasping mist.

The lid came down, and she knelt in the dark, trying to find the anger she needed.

"Now you just stay there," came the creature's voice. "And think about your duties, eh?"

If only she could find the anger. She howled inside her head but made not a whisper. The kist pressed in at her, pushed down on her. The comments from the old wives she pretended not to notice. The gallery men, smirking and laughing and smoking their fat cigars. Her own husband, telling her, "I pay for your clay". *I pay for your clay.* Her muscles trembled. Her fists ached.

"There," whispered Edith McNab. "There's a *good girl.*"

And, at last, Lilian Reid found what she had been reaching for.

#

It was three hours before the roads opened, and Fraser could finally drive their battered old car up the road to the cottage. He was tired, and worried about Lilian; cursing himself for leaving, and thinking on things said and regretted. He opened the front door with some trepidation.

But inside, everything seemed fine. The living room was warm and soft lit, music was playing on the old wireless and, from the kitchen, he heard Lilian singing, and smelled fresh bread and rich soup. As he closed the door, Lilian came through, holding a glass of whisky, and smiled when she saw him.

"Darling!" She gave him a kiss. "They opened the pass! Wonderful. How was your day?"

He smiled back, relieved, and she helped him off with his coat.

"Sit yourself down," she said. "I've got some supper on. Would you like a drink? Here, take mine, I'll get another."

"Lil—" he started, and faltered. "Lil, I'm sorry. The last few days, I've no been…"

She kissed him again. "No," she said, grinning mischievously. "You've not, have you? But you're home now. Sit warm, and I'll be through soon."

He sat, feeling the first sip of whisky burn

in his throat, and relaxed. The room was tidy, and seemed larger, and he wondered if Lilian had moved something out. And it was warm, despite the chill outside. A rich fire roared in the hearth, of black wood that burned with a fierce flame and a scent of camphor, and something faintly familiar too, like ... perfume?

Young Fraser Reid sat and drank his whisky, and watched the fire, and thought idly about how lucky he was; and after a few minutes, he stood up and went to help his wife with supper.

The Children of the Cailleach
D.P. Wilson

They say that something came out of the North Sea before it was the North Sea, long before the vast tsunami which swept the East Coast clean of human life, and it's been living in Banchory Forest ever since. In those days, it was all woods and grassland, and you could walk all the way to Denmark.

Nowadays, everything's penned in by seas and roads and cities, but there are still forests up there which you can wander in 'til you die and whatever lived in them still does. Our people's ancestors called them the *Clann na Cailleach,* but the ancestors of our ancestors had a different name for them. Those folk knew more, and their stories went back to the land under the sea.

Those were the days when you had to travel in groups and be sure to take your spear and your dogs because of the things which lived in the forests.

We find bodies out there, and that's good because we know they haven't been taken. It's when you do sweep-searches for days and find nothing that the fear sets in. The old stories come back to haunt you and a dread of the forest fills you once again. You probably see me as a daft old man, but I was with Search and Rescue for more than twenty years and I don't give a toss what you think: there's something in those woods; it's ancient, it's evil and it takes people.

I bet they wouldn't even let you see the reports; they're all confidential to protect the victims' families. Aye, right. I'll tell you about one we had back in 1989. That's the one when we lost Finlay.

A German family had gone camping in the forest, as they do; always think they know best, and the wife came storming into the police station in Banchory. She'd already been shouting at folk in Auchattie and then turned the wrong way when she crossed the river and driven all the way out to Bridge o' Canny. Anyway, she came in, with the kids, shouting that her husband had run off or fallen into a deer-pit. We laughed at first, mainly at the deer-pit idea, but it turned out he'd only been yards from their tent, getting water from the wee burn they'd camped beside. Ten, fifteen yards, maybe. It had been about seven in the morning and the mist had come rolling in through the night. It was a thick one, and that's what put the first shiver up me and started me thinking of the old tales. Always at night or in the mist.

You've heard o' the Big Grey Man of Ben Macdui? An impossibly tall, spindly, lanky figure that strides around, waving its arms? Well, it's supposed to be like that. Tall, grey, thin, and mad. Maybe that's why it likes the mist? Who knows? None of the stories describe its face.

Maybe it doesn't have one. Or maybe, by the time you're that close, it's too late!

Anyway, the mum told us she and the kids (a girl of nine and a boy of thirteen) had searched and searched for two hours. They'd covered every inch of ground for a quarter-mile round about, and all they'd found was his water-flask.

That's when Finlay Cruickshank piped up, "Yon loon's deid." He told us, "The wifey here's done him in doon the woods an' she's here coverin' her tracks."

There was some laughter but quite a few serious faces. We'd had something similar happen about five years before, that turned out to be a murder. But that was just the start; turned out, the wifey had more English than we'd thought, and she'd got the gist of what Finlay had said. She went ape an' Finlay was on the back foot for sure. He had to back-peddle big-time an' try to calm her down.

"Dinna fash, quine." He was haudin' his palms up. "I didnae mean tae insult ye an', if I did, I'm awfy sorry. Whit I meant wiz we hae tae look intae awthin' here but we'll still be oot searchin' a' the same. There's nae muckle difference when ye're lookin' fir a stiff."

You can only imagine how it went from there, but we eventually got things calmed down and got the details and last known location of the missing person. The teams were called together, and we drove out to the scene, which turned out to be way out past Finzean, up near the Allt Dunnie along Fungle Road. The mist was still down, and the place was disorienting as hell. Creepy, too. No landmarks; just trees everywhere; tall, grey silhouettes in the mist, everywhere you looked.

Thing is; we kept driving and she just

kept saying *No, no*. She had got completely turned around and we ended up taking old forestry tracks as far as the Burn o' Boonie. You can laugh, but it was the boonies, all right; nothing for miles but the forest, flat land and a few streams. If you had one of those to navigate by, you were lucky because they all ended up in the River Dee, eventually.

It was mid-afternoon 'til we found their tent, and the scene was just as she had described, with the little stream about fifteen yards away. The woman showed us where she had found her husband's flask and the kids ran to pick up their Walkmans.

We could see that the ground had been pretty well-trampled all around the tent but, the farther away you got, the fresher things were. Some of us were ghillies and trackers, and we kept everyone else back while we slowly examined the ground in detail, taking our sweet time about it. We worked outwards in a spiral pattern from the tent until we got to the burn, and that's when things started to get weird.

We had identified the husband's tracks and, sure enough, we found some down at the wee stream. They seemed to cross it at one point and start out away from the tent but then they just stopped. I don't mean he stood still or turned around; I mean they simply *disappeared.*

I think Finlay was the first to notice that; he was always the best of us, but he said nothing until Archie Sangster and I also came to a stop and began looking at each other.

"Aye." Finlay said quietly, before getting down on his belly and squinting at the ground all around the area where the tracks stopped.

After about twenty minutes, he stood up and stretched out his back, then he indicated an area and said, "What do you think, boys?"

While Archie and I crawled around on our bellies, Finlay sat down against a tree and rolled a cigarette. He was finished it before we were done.

I couldn't see anything at first but that's because I was looking in the wrong way. I was looking for human or animal tracks; a certain range of shapes and sizes. Things I was familiar with. But, when I simply lay down and looked at the depressions in the turf, I began to see what had got Finlay's attention. There was a series of shallow depressions in the ground, only just visible and about twenty inches long. If you studied them very carefully, they were roughly shaped like a human foot but one that had been distorted in a hall of mirrors; long and narrow. Sometimes you thought you could make out toes; mostly not. They were spaced around three to four yards apart; that was the step-length, right to left and they appeared to be coming in from the far reaches of the forest. They stopped about five yards from where the husband's prints disappeared and then turned around and made back in roughly the direction they had come. Were they deeper, like whatever made them was carrying something? Maybe.

All three of us exchanged long looks before anyone said anything.

"We have to follow it." Finlay was the first to speak, but he wasn't giving much away.

Another short silence before I said, "Aye."

Archie just nodded. We were all very subdued and I could see the colour of the other two had drained a bit.

The first sweep-search had been organised and was heading out at 90 degrees to our direction, so help wouldn't be that far away.

"My gun's in the Jeep." Finlay said and, once his deer-rifle was over his shoulder, we all set out in line-abreast. I carried a big skinning-knife and I know Archie did, too. The going was very slow, and no one said a word as we tried to follow the nearly non-existent trail. I had a tingle between the shoulder blades and a creepy feeling of being watched. The other two were glancing over their shoulders more than usual and walking hunched-up and sullen. We had all grown up around here and I know we were all thinking along similar lines, but no one would say it.

The thick mist hadn't lifted all day and it had taken us more than an hour to cover about a mile through the forest. Now that we knew what we were looking for, the trail wasn't impossible, but it was still faint and difficult, making for slow-going. The day was wearing on and I had begun thinking about the dark.

"Anyone bring a torch?" I asked in a quiet voice. They were the first words any of us had spoken since we started out. Finlay gave a little snort of laughter.

"Aye," he said. Archie shook his head.

"That's one of us, then," I commented, and Finlay gave a faint smile;

"Frightened of the dark?" he taunted, "Scared the Bogle will get you?"

In all honesty I was, but I wasn't going to admit that here, to these men. Perhaps I should have but it was Archie who replied.

"It's no a Bogle, Finlay!" he hissed. Then, even quieter, "You know you shouldn't joke about *na daoine de'n choille!*"

"Wheesht, man!" Finlay snapped. He looked angry, but whether at Archie or himself was impossible to tell.

I was still surprised at what I had just heard. Around here, we don't usually talk about them and, if we do, we almost never name them. The only times I had heard them referred to by the oldsters, they had been called *Clann na Cailleach,* Children of the Hag, but what Archie had said was different. It was Gaelic, all right, but it meant 'The Children of the Forest'. Was that an older name? From a time before the old Celtic Gods held sway over the north? Finlay was angry and Archie looked embarrassed, so I did as I always do and kept my mouth shut. Whatever we were tracking, it certainly wasn't a child.

After another hour, the light was beginning to fade and we thought about turning back. We should have, but the trail was still leading us on and we knew that, by morning, it would have all but vanished, so we exchanged glances but no one said a word and we pressed on.

An hour after that, it was fully dark and we were tracking by torchlight, which isn't as difficult as it sounds; if you hold the torch close to the ground and shine its light at a shallow angle, it can actually cause prints to stand out even more. At any rate, we were no slower. What's more, the mist appeared to have thinned a little and there was a full moon. Its light permeated the mist and made it glow. I don't know if you've ever seen that happen, but it can be quite magical. That night however, it was plain creepy.

Eventually, even going slow and using the torch, we lost the trail. Nothing mysterious; the ground just got harder and the trail fainter until none of us could make out anything at all. I, for one, was secretly relieved; no one had seen tracks like that before and we all had a foreboding at the back of our minds that we wouldn't put into words.

We sat down and scratched our heads, and I was about to say, "Let's call it a day," when Finlay beat me to the punch.

"I say we head one more mile on the last bearing and then call it a day."

Archie and I looked at each other and then reluctantly nodded. It was the worst decision I ever made. We ploughed on for quite a while until, eventually, I began to feel distinctly ill-at-ease. Looking at the others' faces, I could tell that they were feeling the same thing, but still no one said a word.

We could see a change in the quality of the light ahead and then, all of a sudden, literally from one step to the next, I was filled with an overwhelming dread. I can't describe it any better than to say it was sheer, unreasoning terror. It swept over us from nowhere, occasioned by nothing.

At the same moment, we could see that the light was changing, because we were stepping out into a clearing in the forest, maybe a hundred yards across. In the weird glow of the mist, we could see a tarn in front of us: a wee lochan, perhaps half the width of the clearing and, at the opposite side of the lochan was a small knoll, perhaps thirty feet in height.

The lochan had an unnaturally dark appearance and the knoll had the size and shape of what we often called a *cnoc nan sithiean,* or fairy mound, (there are still farmers in these parts who won't set iron to the ground in such a place) except that it wore a jagged crown of dead and broken trees. Even the grass that covered it had a dark and unhealthy appearance and the water in the lochan looked somehow thick and oily.

There was a sound like wind in the trees, but the mist wasn't moving. Finlay shone his torch upward; everything looked so still and that whistling now sounded like distant screaming: there were almost words.

I thought I could make out a faraway and drawn-out, *"Hilfe! Hilfe!"*

Then a deeper voice, right behind us, said, *"Hilfe."* And laughed.

We whipped around but there was nothing there. When Archie and I turned back, Finlay was gone, his torch lying on the wet ground. Our eyes had been off him for only two or three seconds. There had been no sound, no scream; nothing.

I picked up his torch and shouted, "Finlay!" at the top of my lungs and, as Archie followed suit, I caught a glimpse of movement on top of the mound. It was anything but clear, but I swear it looked like an impossibly tall, implausibly spindly being, climbing down, into the ground, waving its arms in a hideous frenzy.

There was nowhere near us for anyone or anything to hide or run to. It was completely impossible for Finlay to hide or have been hidden during the time he was out of our sight.

Then, the worst of all: Finlay's voice, in that awful whistling-sound. There were only three words, but they got louder and louder, as if the source of the voice was rushing towards us.

The last words I heard Finlay Cruickshank utter were, "Run! Run! *Run!*"

To our everlasting shame, we did just that; we bolted. I held Finlay's torch and we weren't tracking anything, now. We ran back the way we had come and there was a loud, deep groan, like a ship's timbers about to burst. It sounded as if it came from *under the ground,* beneath our feet and we couldn't seem to reach the timberline at the edge of the clearing.

"Come on!" I gasped and pushed Archie between his shoulders.

I had never seen my friend's face contorted like that before; it was deeply shocking. I'm telling you, we sprinted for a good five minutes without ever getting any closer to the trees, while the laughing and groaning came from beneath and behind us. It was only when, in a last desperate and unconscious act, I grabbed Archie's hand and we struggled together, that we were suddenly among trees. Not just among trees but a good half of the way back to where we had started, at that poor German family's tent.

Not long before we reached it, we heard

people calling our names and we answered with more relief than I have words to express. It was the others. They had completed a big sweep-search, covering one whole quadrant of the designated area. They found nothing.

When they inevitably asked us where Finlay had got to, Archie and I exchanged a glance;

"We got separated around three miles out," I said. "I don't think any of us know that part of the country well; we're more from the east of here."

There is an unwritten rule in Search and Rescue that you don't talk about the weird things (and there are more of those than you might think) except after a few pints at the Christmas do and then only to close friends.

The guys went into a huddle and the only ghillie from out that way told us, "There's a lot of bogs and sink-holes out there. How well does Finlay know the land?"

"About as well as we do," I replied and the ghillie sighed.

"Bugger." He decided, "We'd better do a search. Do you two know where you separated?"

Now I could be confident.

"Yes." I replied, "We've got known bearings

and distances; we can go straight there."

So, we headed back into that endless forest, feeling a little better now that we had the numbers on our side. Everyone had a head-torch as well as a hand-held lamp and we made plenty of noise, which kept our spirits up. We reversed our bearings and headed straight for the dark lochan with its menacing mound, walking line-abreast so that we spread out over a third of a mile as we advanced.

To cut a long story short, we didn't find it; not that night, the next day, nor any of the next three days. A helicopter was called in from RAF Lossiemouth and it spent the best part of a day 'mowing the lawn' over the entire area. There was no clearing, no lochan, no mound.

Now I understood the look the local ghillie had given me when I had described the eerie clearing and its mysterious *cnoc*. He knew this land as well as I know my own patch and he had never seen the place.

Despite repeated searches, we never found Finlay's remains nor those of the German tourist.

Archie and I came in for quite a bit of ribbing because of our police report which had to state at least the bare facts in terms of times, distances, and locations. The younger guys would wave their hands and go, "Woo-hoo-hoo!"

Then, sure enough, at the Christmas do, I ended up having to tell the story again. This time to an audience of two: a police inspector who had more than a passing acquaintance with macabre tales, and an old-time Search and Rescue team-mate, Donald Gunn, who was retiring that night.

Donald's face had gone almost white when I got to the part about the menacing clearing and the *cnoc,* with its broken crown of dead trees and he abruptly got up and walked away as I began describing what we heard and saw there. The local gossip was that Donny's father had been a drunk and, one night, he'd gone wandering off into the forest. The sixteen-year-old Donny had run after him when he found out but had returned in the morning, alone. Donny's father was never seen again and Donny himself had been a slightly subdued individual ever since.

Later, when I found him outside and we ransacked my crumpled pack of cigarettes, I thought he looked more relaxed than I had ever seen him; almost relieved. I put it down to his retirement until he placed a hand, which was still very strong, on my arm, looked me straight in the eye, and said quietly, "Don't ever talk about it and pray you never find that place again."

And, with that, he was gone, into the raucous throng.

The Fabric of Time
Clare Marsh

We edged the car down the steep main street of Robin Hood's Bay, avoiding the crowds of day trippers who stepped off the pavement into our path. The road ran out where the high tide lapped at the slipway. Our detailed instructions were to double back up the cobbled lane to the side. I jumped out to collect the key to Harbour Cottage from the Old Neptune pub two doors down.

My heart sank when I unlocked the front door and we stood in the only downstairs room – I instantly knew what kind of week we'd have. It was not as described in the holiday brochure. For 'quaint' read 'cramped'. My husband, Dan, at over six-foot-tall, was already muttering ominously.

The so-called easy chairs looked anything but, and there'd be no room for his long legs to stretch out. Then he bumped his head going up the tight staircase with our luggage.

"I bet the brochure didn't describe the décor as 'tired?" he moaned.

I tried to jolly him along but, when we looked into the wet room and discovered mould, I gave up.

"We must move the car to the top of the hill to park as it's blocking the road," I said.

In the car park we didn't get out and argued about our options.

"I'm tempted to pack up and ask for a full refund," Dan said.

"But I've always wanted to stay in Robin Hood's Bay. Look how close we are to the sea." I tried, as usual, to be positive.

"And did you notice that strange smell around the stairs?" he asked.

"What do you expect in such an old house? The place has real character, it's a fisherman's cottage." My phone rang. I looked at the number and put it on speaker. It was Miss Holmes, the property owner.

She'd been in contact several times since I made the booking.

"I hope you're both settling in? Is the

property to your liking?"

"Yes, thank you." I'm always placatory. I can't stand conflict. I didn't like to say the photos had obviously been taken a very long while ago and the whole place needed redecoration.

Then, Dan intervened and didn't hold back, listing the issues he'd found. "There are light bulbs out on both staircases; the shower room is in an appalling state; there's clutter everywhere and a horrible smell."

Miss Holmes blustered, "Shelley at the pub was meant to clean the property before you arrived. I'll call her to fix those things." She hung up.

"Looks like you've already decided to stay," Dan sighed. "Oh well, it's only for a week and we should be out most of the time. We'll only have to sleep there."

"Actually, that top floor bedroom is the best part of the property with that stunning sea view. We won't get that anywhere else for the same price this week at no notice."

We walked back down to the sea, browsing the shop windows, and bought ice creams. Everything always feels better after an ice cream. A sign board at the slipway advertised 'Ghost Tour tonight 7.30pm'.

"Let's go on that," I suggested. Dan didn't take much persuading. My phone rang –

Miss Holmes again.

"I've been in touch with Shelley. She'll come in on Monday to have another clean. She said she'd done it thoroughly today. There are lightbulbs in the cupboard under the stairs if you want to replace them. Strange though, they blew last week. No life in the damned things nowadays."

"Thank you, we'll do that."

"Do you have any plans for this evening?"

"We fancied joining the ghost walk."

"You really shouldn't." Miss Holmes sounded breathless. "I'm not sure that's such a good idea."

"Why not?"

"Just don't believe everything you hear – it's a lot of silly nonsense." And she cut the line again.

We picked up fish and chips and climbed the coast path to eat it on a bench.

"What do you make of Miss Holmes?" Dan asked.

"I believe she's well-intentioned, but anyone would think she was anxious about something."

"Probably her reviews and ratings. Let's face it: they're somewhat mixed."

That was a dig at me. Apparently, it was all my fault I'd booked without reading them. This was a hastily arranged holiday at the end of a trying summer. Usually my research is meticulous, but not this time. Scrolling through properties I came across Harbour Cottage. While it was tiny, there should have been enough room for the two of us for a brief holiday. And it came at a surprisingly good price, which dipped dramatically for this week before going up by two hundred pounds for the next. Strange for mid-September. Of course, it was old and looked as if it needed updating, but I'd sold it to Dan on the basis of its charm or, more likely, the pub next door.

Wearing warm clothes for the September evening, we joined the crowd at the slipway. Our host arrived with a flourish, in a black cloak and carrying a flickering lantern. After a stirring introduction we followed her up into the town, where we made frequent stops to hear chilling stories.

I nudged Dan. "Wouldn't it be a laugh if she stops outside our place and it turns out it's haunted?"

"Hysterical, I don't think!"

We walked in small groups through the labyrinth of narrow streets, hearing tales of smugglers and murders. Then we arrived outside the Old Neptune.

"Right, so we're staying next to a spooky

pub – great!" Dan said.

But no, our guide walked up past the pub and stopped outside our front door.

"Oh no." I gripped Dan's arm. "Just our luck. I won't be able to forget this story all week!"

"In the 1870s, William Levitt lived in Harbour cottage," said our guide. "He owned a fishing boat and his crew were from the village. His fiancée, Ellen Harland, lived at the Old Neptune Inn." She pointed to the pub. "There was a terrible storm and his fishing boat was due to dock at Whitby to unload its catch. When it was a week overdue, Ellen was frantic with worry and word reached her that the boat had foundered on the rocks with no survivors. Ellen was such a frail little thing. On hearing the shocking news, she shut herself in Harbour Cottage. Her anguished cries could be heard along the lane that night. She was discovered dead at the bottom of the stairs the next morning, on what should have been their wedding day."

"Great, so Ellen died in our house? I don't think I'm going to get much sleep tonight," I muttered to Dan. But, despite our reservations, we both slept well. I'm not sure whether it was the sea air that knocked us out or, more likely, the bottle of red wine we consumed after the ghost walk to steady our nerves. The weather at the start of our stay was delightful, blue skies and perfect conditions for long walks. We made the most of the coastline and took the steam train to Whitby. The openly gothic character of the town put our own feeble fears in the shade.

Shelley came in to clean on Monday. She apologised and said that it was a never-ending job with the cottage, despite its tiny size. However much she cleaned – and she had on our arrival day – mould would instantly appear in the shower cubicle and the crockery always seemed tainted. It must be that the old building was damp. She also mentioned a strange smell in the back of the cupboard under the stairs, not helped by all the clutter. Had we noticed? She had to change the air fresheners weekly.

"You replaced the lightbulbs yourselves? If I had a pound for every time I've had to do that..."

"It must be faulty electrics," Dan said, ever practical and rational.

The weather unexpectedly deteriorated on Thursday, so we visited the museum to learn more about local history and its seafaring connections. We descended into a small room, labelled The Old Mortuary, where the temperature was noticeably colder. A display of navy-blue sweaters caught my eye. I do some knitting and was admiring the skill that went into making them.

The curator came into the room and saw my interest.

"Women knitted these 'ganseys', and each coastal village had its own distinctive pattern," he said. "If a body washed up after too long in the sea, there would be inevitable damage, making identification impossible – the decaying bodies would be kept cool here in this mortuary. You can feel how well ventilated it is."

I remembered stopping outside here on the ghost walk and I shivered. 'So, where do the ganseys come in?'

'Their unique patterns meant if a body washed up after a shipwreck it was possible to locate exactly where they came from, even if the face of the drowned man had been obliterated by time and tide. And fish, of course. Look, here's the Robin Hood's Bay example." He pointed to the unique combination of twisted cables and moss stitch panels.

I took a picture with my phone, then asked about the rings hanging on the wall, tied with dangling shreds of faded fabric.

"And what are these?"

"Maiden's Garlands, or virgin's crowns. They were considered a symbol of purity. That's another local tradition, going back many centuries, created when an unmarried woman died. Their family and friends would attach strips of material, sometimes gloves, to a hoop and they would be carried at the front of the funeral procession. Afterwards they were displayed in the church over the family's pew. You should look up the hill in Fylingdales church – we have a fine collection there."

And I thought of poor Ellen, who died just before her wedding. Perhaps she had a Maiden's Garland made for her?

The bar was full for a quiz that Thursday night at the Old Neptune. I noticed an ancient embroidery sampler on the wall and deciphered Ellen's name. When I asked Shelley about her, she said she was an ancestral aunt.

"I have her diary which she kept during the last year of her life. It makes sad reading when you know what happened next."

"I'd be interested to hear her story in her own words. I understand she died in Harbour Cottage?"

"That's right. It's a tragic tale. You can borrow it if you promise to return it when you leave."

Although the quiz was highly competitive, my mind kept wandering to the handwritten book in my bag. When we got back, Dan said he was going to turn in, while I decided to look at the diary. Just before he went upstairs, Dan paused.

"That smell is definitely getting worse. I really must phone Miss Holmes to complain."

As I settled down to read, I could hear the last pub customers clatter down the lane, then there was silence apart from the increasing wind. Ellen's diary was mostly factual. While her days in the Old Neptune didn't vary, she recorded special occasions. On January 1st she made some resolutions. She would be neat in her appearance, work harder and without complaint, and knit more to earn money in her spare time. In fact, she listed the progress of the sweaters she produced and who they were for. She took two weeks to complete them, no doubt fitting this around her duties at the inn.

Valentine's Day contained the words *William proposed to me. I said yes, over and over.* They marked their betrothal a few days later with both families celebrating. The diary entries then look forward to their marriage on September 18th. Ellen listed items she acquired for her trousseau. They planned to make Harbour Cottage their home, which William rented next to the Old Neptune. In August Ellen noted that she had finished making William his *wedding gansey*. She was proud of her handiwork and wrote *it is the best I ever made*. Throughout the year Ellen also expressed fears for the future. In January, she had noted a coughing fit and discovered blood on her pillow. She made red marks in the diary to signify this each time it happened, and bouts became increasingly frequent. I feared she had the first signs of consumption. She would never have made old bones.

I tried to imagine William in this little house, making it comfortable for his intended. Chopping wood for the fire, doing repairs, keeping it shipshape. And then there would be his times away on the unforgiving North Sea, sailing his fishing boat after the shoals of herring. I must have drifted off as, when I woke, the wind had got up and was howling around the bay. The Old Neptune sign creaked. Then came the rain and, looking out of the window, the cobbled lane had disappeared under the torrent cascading down to the harbour. A solitary man was battling up from the slipway - trudging doggedly in heavy boots, bent against the wind and rain. It was a filthy night to be outdoors, and I hoped he got home soon. I let the curtain fall back.

As I was halfway up the stairs, the bulb went out, plunging me into darkness and causing me to trip. I yelled as my ankle give way. Dan appeared from the bedroom rubbing his eyes. He led me back downstairs and settled me in a chair with my foot elevated and a bag of frozen peas on it. He opened the cupboard under the stairs to search for yet another replacement bulb.

"I swear the smell in here is getting worse."

"Maybe it's a dead mouse?"

"No, it smells more like rotting seaweed. I'm going to pull everything out..." He rummaged around, dragging out jumbled items. He eventually reached a wooden box. "I think it's coming from in here. Maybe kids staying here previously left some dead crabs in it for a laugh?" He pulled it out and set it on the floor in front of me. "Well, it's pretty old and the clasp is rusty."

"So it can't be kids. That hasn't been open for years," I said.

Dan used a kitchen knife to prise it open. It released a nauseating smell. Inside was a solitary lace glove, yellowed with age. I dug deeper and discovered a gansey sweater – which had the tell-tale twisted cables and panels of moss stitch. I checked it with the picture on my phone – its owner had come from Robin Hood's Bay. It was soaking wet, not just damp, and smelt of mould and wool and rotting fish. I had my suspicions what the items were – whose they were – but the pain from my ankle was overwhelming and I just wanted to get to bed. I asked Dan to replace them as he found them.

Friday morning was overcast and, although I was sure my ankle wasn't broken, I didn't want to walk far. I hobbled down to the beach and set myself up with a folding chair and flask. Dan went off for a cliff walk. I'd brought Ellen's diary in the beach bag and wanted to read more. I realised that the anniversary of the date she'd marked for her marriage, 18th September, was the next day, Saturday – the day we were due to leave. On 10th September she wrote *I saw William off, his last trip before our wedding. I was sad to see him go, but I can't wait to become his wife.* I pictured her keeping herself busy with wedding preparations: feeling happy, and perhaps nervous, at the prospect.

On 12th September, the tone suddenly changed. *William should have returned home by now. There was a fearful storm last night. I do hope he put into the shelter of the land safely.* By 13th, her fears were increasing, and the entry for 14th was *No word of my dear William. I pray God he put in at Whitby.* The next day she wrote *There are rumours of a wreck along the coast. Still no sign of William.* Poor Ellen not knowing for certain what happened. On 16th September *Terrible news, wreckage from my William's boat has been washed up in the bay. Hope is fading.*

I suggested we should take the garments up to the museum to see if the curator could shed any light on their age. We must have made a strange sight, me limping and Dan carrying the old wooden chest. The curator was interested in the clothes.

"Fabrics often don't last, but the gansey was tightly knitted to be weatherproof. It was definitely made in Robin Hood's Bay," he said. "That lace glove is so delicate and might have been for a wedding."

"How old do you think they are?" I asked.

"I can't be sure, but from the wooden chest probably mid to late 19th century."

We took them back to the house as they belonged to Miss Holmes. I rang her that evening to tell her what we found.

"That's a special box, you had no right to open it and pry." She sounded angry.

"Ok, ok sorry, but there was such a dreadful smell coming from that cupboard and the light still keeps going out on the stairs."

I thought she said something like, "This is always such a difficult time of year," before the line abruptly went dead.

On the way up to bed this time the light bulb on the stairs exploded, showering us with glass.

"Mind your hands: there are shards everywhere," Dan said, as he shone a torch around.

"Let's leave it until morning."

I couldn't sleep, although Dan snored soundly, so I read Ellen's diary again. I hadn't looked beyond the date of her proposed marriage, assuming there would be no more entries, but, at the end of the year, there was different handwriting.

This was the year we lost our poor Ellen. She was buried on 22nd September, four days after what should have been her wedding day. Such a shocking waste. All the village turned out to see her and William buried. Her in her new dress and him in the wedding gansey she made him. We made a Maiden's Garland for her as a reminder with one of her gloves. We never could find the other.

And I felt queasy. Suppose the gansey downstairs wasn't the wedding one – I now knew William had been buried in that. So, could it be the one he drowned in? I stared out at the full moon reflected on the bay. A movement in the corner of my eye drew my attention. A figure, the same as last night, trudged up the hill. He certainly kept late hours. I could hear the drag of his boots on the cobbles and expected him to pass, but no, his footsteps stopped outside the cottage. He disappeared from view, then I heard scuffling in the porch. I shook Dan awake.

"There's a drunk outside. He's trying to get in. I saw him at the same time last night."

"Probably nothing to worry about then. The door's bolted, isn't it?"

"I thought you'd locked up earlier?"

"No, I thought you had."

"In that case he only has to turn the handle and he'll be in."

We both raced to the top of the stairs and looked down and gasped in horror. The doorway was filled by a large figure. Pools of water collected at his feet. He was saturated. I could smell the stench of the sea and fish and fear. His eyes seemed to be searching for something or someone.

He spotted the chest, in the centre of the room and no longer hidden in the back of the cupboard.

"At last," he groaned. Lifting his arms, he took off his gansey and placed it inside and took the out the lace glove which he held to his battered, disfigured face. His sobs will haunt me for the rest of my life.

I found myself saying, "Take the glove, William."

He turned and made to leave, whispering, "Ellen, my love where are you?"

"She's waiting for you," I said.

Dan and I clung onto each other, shaking. We knew instinctively he meant us no harm. This was the scenario he'd been fated to play out repeatedly on this date until his soul could get some rest. I prayed finding the wedding glove might give him some peace. He went to the door and, when we looked up and down the lane, he had disappeared.

The next morning, I returned the house key to Shelley and thanked her for the loan of the diary.

"Was everything alright for the rest of your stay?"

"We had a very strange experience last night."

"Did our William pay you a visit?" she asked.

"How did you know?"

"He often does this time of year. Between his death and the wedding that never happened."

"Have you ever seen him?"

"No, but Miss Holmes said she did once and she's never been the same since. She really shouldn't let the cottage this week in September, even at such a reduced rate. Leave the house well alone for the spirits, I say."

On our way out of the village, we stopped at Old St Stephen's Church. Inside were the faded Maiden's Garlands – one had been labelled for Ellen Harland with her dates. In the centre was the other white lace glove she would have worn to her wedding. Its twin had been in the chest at Harbour Cottage until William had taken it away with him last night. We walked around the graveyard searching for their final resting place and found two lichen covered stones next to each other. The weathered writing confirmed they belonged to William and Ellen, with their epitaph *Parted in Life, United in Death.* I placed a bunch of Michaelmas Daisies and lavender I'd picked from the little back garden of Harbour Cottage on their graves, where a lace glove rested on the soil.

As we pulled away in our car, I was busy consulting the map.

"And what review should we give the cottage on Trip Advisor?" asked Dan.

The Night Shift
John Matthews
3rd Place

I switched off the car engine and *Wizzard*, who still wished it could be Christmas everyday, ceased playing from the radio. The relief from this was replaced by the sound of the wind hurling flakes of snow at the windscreen of my car.

It was going to be a white Christmas, I guessed.

My hands still gripped the steering wheel as I stared into the black, deserted car park. Unlike Wizzard, I didn't wish it could be Christmas every day, right now. I was fed up with everyone's smiling faces and their endless chatter...

Not long to the big day now...

Are you all set for Christmas..?

Are you and Hayley doing anything nice for Christmas?

It was Christmas Eve tomorrow and I still hadn't got her a present.

Snow began to build up on the windows of my car. I could just about see out through the remaining bits of clear glass as the snowflakes swirled around in the light coming from the top of the lamp posts. The Christmas card scene was broken by a young couple, making a dash from the supermarket to their car, grocery bags weighing them down. Their excited squeals heightened as they tried to run across the car park in tiny steps. Then it got even louder when they couldn't open their car but, at last, the right button was pressed and they dived in, covered in snow. I looked across at them as they brushed the snow off each other, illuminated by their interior car light, still smiling and giggling. That could have been me and Hayley, but our relationship wasn't fun anymore.

It was becoming a burden.

Hayley was the supermarket's front-end manager, and we had connected at last year's staff Christmas party. It wasn't that

I no longer loved her, just it was a struggle for me to summon the effort to do anything nice for her. The fact that I was now keeping things from her didn't help either, and I think she sensed that. Life was consuming me, and I didn't know how to make it stop.

I let go of the steering wheel and zipped my coat up, bracing myself for the wintry night on the other side of the car door, before taking one last look around the car park.

At this time of night, the staff vehicles outnumber the shoppers and, as I had recently been promoted to night crew manager, I recognised the cars which belonged to my staff. As usual, they had all beaten me to our nine o'clock start but at least no one seemed to be missing. The last thing I wanted was someone pulling a sickie. The shelves inside would already be stripped bare by the ravenous Christmas shoppers, and it was my job to ensure we filled them back up again.

Hang on. No Andy though? But he was often later than me.

The couple who had dashed from the supermarket drove past in their snow-covered car and I momentarily followed their taillights around the car park. I wished I hadn't. As the taillights disappeared into the blizzard, there it was. At first, it was just a blur, but I did a second take. Definitely a Volvo shape; several rows over from me; in a lonely parking bay. My heart sank.

I couldn't check the registration or any other details as the snow was not letting up, but it was just the right shape or, from my point of view, the wrong one. The rectangle tank shape just sat there, taking the full brunt of the snowstorm. It was an old-style Volvo and it belonged to Michael.

I slumped forward, my forehead resting on the top of the steering wheel. Not tonight, please.

Despite being night crew manager and Michael's boss, I still had no say in the nights he worked and that was starting to bug me. If he was in tonight, I would have to deal with it and manage the best I could.

I took a deep breath and pushed myself back upright. My hand was about to reach for the door handle when it stopped. I had to have another look. I wiped the windscreen in a vain attempt to get a better view. I thought I saw him as an interior light briefly came on, but I could have been mistaken.

I rubbed my temples with my fingertips. The past few months have been traumatic. I just needed to get through Christmas then take a break from all this. I could maybe take Hayley somewhere nice. It could even be part of her Christmas present.

The snow continued to fill up the windscreen and I was going to have to get out. I steeled myself, reached for the handle once more, then hauled myself out into the winter's night.

My face instantly numbed. The warmth from the car was swept away as I struggled to pull the collar up on my coat. Snow bombarded me as I clicked the car shut and I made for the front doors of the supermarket, head down. I didn't look towards the Volvo.

"Hi, boss."

My heart jolted as I looked down. A pair of boots had joined me in the snow. It was Michael but I kept walking; still head down. So, he was in tonight again. He had been in the last three nights. Surely he was due a night off?

"Some night, eh, boss? Just as well we are going inside."

I was struggling to breathe in the wind, never mind hold a conversation, as the snow lashed around me. I could hardly see where I was placing my feet now as I quickened my pace and crossed where I thought the zebra should be. Without looking up, I headed for the front doors.

"Is Andy late again, boss?"

Andy? Probably, I guessed.

The supermarket doors slid open and the heaters above the doors in the foyer attacked the layer of snow on my coat. I stopped to warm up and, almost at once, water appeared around my feet. Michael didn't hang around to warm up though and disappeared inside.

A group of carol singers were dismantling song sheet stands, collecting their discarded coats and rattling the contents of their collection tins. Their clothes were decorated with flashing ties, bits of tinsel and silly headwear. Their ordeal was over, mine was just about to begin and I fingered the foil strip of pills in my jacket pocket.

I had liked Michael when we both started our employment at the supermarket, just over a year ago. His mate, Andy, as well. As three new staff we were thrown together, but it soon became apparent that me and Michael were never going to become friends. We both had one eye on the night crew manager's position that was up for grabs the following September, when the person that already held that position was due to retire. Andy though, was just happy to have a job. His ambitions lay outside work, as a musician. So, watch out, Ed Sheeran. But me and Michael? Well... we were a ticking time bomb.

I stamped my feet and walked past the carol singers, through the next set of sliding doors. The Christmas scene continued inside. Giant red and gold baubles hung from the ceiling, bobbing about in the draught from the door. Interspersed between the baubles were huge Christmas grocery signs, with smiling elves and snowmen on them. Directing you not to miss bargains. Staff wore Santa hats, flashing earrings, and those ridiculous head bopper things. A huge tree dominated the kiosk area with gifts donated by customers for underprivileged, local children.

I hurried on as I wanted to speak to Hayley, but the service desk was closing down and she was too busy sorting out her staff on the checkouts to notice me. Her shapely figure, blonde, bobbed hair, and that cheeky smile. God, I'm such a fool.

I tried to catch Hayley's eye once more, but Michael was now by her side.

What was his game? Can't have my job so he wants my girlfriend instead? I hated him but I didn't want to cause another scene. So, I walked down the health and beauty aisle, past the half empty shelves and paused briefly by the fragrances. The scent engulfed my nostrils making me feel giddy. Maybe I could get Hayley some perfume.

I stood for a while picking up some bottles, removing the tops and sniffing them. The first one I tried smelled like fruity sweets, the next, a vanilla pod. The third bottle I picked up smelled of rose petals.

God, this is difficult. I was no good at making decisions.

Some of my staff were already wheeling pallets full of groceries onto the shop floor, eager to make inroads into the night that lay ahead. I said *hello* to a couple of them, as I decided perfume wasn't a great idea and I started to make my way up the aisle to see Sue, the store manager, for tonight's handover.

"Hi, boss. What do you want me to make a start on?"

Michael startled me again. He had a habit of doing that. Sneaking up on you when you least expected it. I knew what he would like to do though, like most nights, it would be one of the easier jobs no doubt.

"There is a lot of cardboard already, boss. I could start by putting it in the baler for you?"

Easy job it was then.

Michael didn't wait to get permission and

headed off to the warehouse. My head felt light, and I touched the strip of pills in my coat pocket again, before letting them go.

I still had 12 hours to get through.

I left the shop floor behind and headed down the corridor to the manager's office; knocked on the door; and went in.

"Ah," Sue said, coat already on. "I was just about to phone you. I thought you weren't coming in again. How are you?"

Flaming awful, I wanted to scream.

"I'm good," I said. "Just a bit tired with it being Christmas and that."

"Well, only one shift to go," Sue said. "Then Christmas will be over, and we can review your trial period as night crew manager, which shouldn't be a problem."

I paused... Trial period?

"I take it there are no problems anymore?" Sue continued.

Problems? Where do I start? I felt the strip of pills in my pocket again.

"No problems," I said. "I take it you have none with me now." This time her pause was too long.

"Nothing that can't wait, and you are the last person that needs to be reminded what a terrible year it's been, so let's just get through Christmas first, then we can all move forward together."

Smalltalk over, we then ran through the handover for the night ahead.

"The tannoy system is on the blink again," Sue said finally, as she headed for the door. "So there is an electrician due at 6 o'clock tomorrow morning, to have another look at it."

"No worries," I said, and I waved her goodbye.

With Sue gone, I headed to the canteen. It was well past nine now, but I needed caffeine. Several smiling faces headed in the opposite direction, their shifts over. Soon, the only people in the huge supermarket building would be me and a handful of my staff.

I walked into the canteen and, as usual at this hour, it was empty. The only sounds were the hum of the refrigerators and the vending machines. The lights were all off except the one by the machines. I had just pressed black, one sugar, when the tannoy crackled.

"Night crew manager required in the warehouse. Second call."

Second call? Flaming tannoy, I hadn't even heard the first one. I waited for my coffee and pressed a couple of white tablets into my hand from the strip that had been in my pocket.

Several gulps later, I was back on the shop floor, giving instructions to my staff for the night ahead. They were annoyed that they couldn't play their music over the tannoy system tonight, as it was on the blink again. My suggestion that it was working two minutes ago when I had been summoned to the warehouse was ridiculed and met with, *we never heard anything.*

My staff, many of whom I worked alongside before my promotion, were on the whole okay now I was their boss, but I had heard rumours of discontent about me lately that I needed to address.

He spends more time in that office of his, than helping us.

Found him in the warehouse. God knows what he had been doing in there all this time. Talking to himself again no doubt.

He's not been the same since… you know.

I headed for the warehouse and the doors opened automatically as I approached them. I walked in, past my office and headed on through the maze of pallets to the back of the warehouse. A faulty strip light, halfway down, flickered and shadows were cast around some pallets, creating pockets of darkness. This didn't bother me though because I was fixated on the back of the warehouse, and I kept walking towards the rear as I knew what I would find when I got there...

Michael and the great big hunk of orange steel that was the cardboard baler machine.

"Boss, the machine is jammed again. Think it's the baler rope at the back that has come off again. Do you want me to go inside the machine and sort it out for you?"

This was now becoming a regular occurrence. It happened every night Michael and Andy worked together.

To re-attach the baler rope you had to open the huge metal door at the front of the baler machine and then re-thread it using a long metal pole. But it was easier and quicker if you got inside the baler machine and did this by hand. But this unticked the health and safety box.

"Well, boss? Shall I?" Michael said.

Why did a simple thing like a rope that went around the cardboard bales always foul up? The machine was otherwise so easy to operate. You threw the cardboard in the empty side, dragged over the crushing plate on rollers and pressed the bale button. The metal plate would then lower into the machine to crush the cardboard.

I stood staring at the machine. I could feel my eyes filling and, before I knew it, my chest heaved up and down. The pills hadn't had time to kick in yet.

"I'll go inside then, boss," Michael said. Like he had done three months ago...

Michael had opened the door and climbed inside. The metal plate was already above his head. It should have been on the other side.

"It's this one that's come off. Watch the door for me will you, in case it slams shut," he had said.

I had stood staring at the chest high, bright orange door, motionless.

Michael had been getting on my nerves. Always having an excuse to chat with Hayley. Making her laugh and feel alive.

"I think that's that one sorted. Just checking the other one," he had continued,

It wasn't like I had caught them in bed or anything, but Hayley was different with Michael. I had sensed a chemistry.

We are just workmates, Hayley had said when I confronted her.

"Yes, this one's off as well." Michael had said.

Then there was the night crew manager's job which had been coming up. I had needed that extra money to impress Hayley. What had Michael wanted the money for?

He was still living at home with his parents.

"Got it. Nearly done," he had said, from inside the baler machine

When I had applied for the night crew manager's job, I had heard Michael was favourite to get it. I had to do something. What if he was caught doing something he shouldn't have been doing? Like being inside a machine he had strictly been told not to. I know everybody did it, but rules are rules.

"There. Sorted," he had said, still inside the orange baler machine.

I had stared at the orange door long enough and I slammed it shut.

"Hey. What the..?"

I had then pressed the bale button for a nanosecond and a piercing scream came from within.

"Let me out! Let me out," he had yelled.

The plate had barely moved an inch, but it was enough to scare the crap out of him.

"The door is jammed Michael, the wind must have caught it," I had lied. "I will get help."

But the bale light was still flashing, waiting for someone to complete the bale.

So, I switched the baler machine off at the wall, just to be safe.

"Come back. Let me out, let me out," he had pleaded.

All I had needed to do now was alert the retiring night crew manager to the danger Michael had put himself in. Perfect.

I remembered walking calmly to the night crew office to put a call out for the manager. From there I could stop anyone walking into the warehouse to use the machine and collar the night crew manager when he got here.

I think Michael is trapped inside the baler machine, I would say.

"Night crew manager to the warehouse please," I had shouted over the tannoy.

Michael was screaming the place down, but I knew the night crew manager must be on his way by now. My plan had been fool proof and it would have worked...

Except for Andy.

Andy – I want to be like Ed Sheeran – Andy. Working away at the back of the warehouse. Earbuds in and out of our view, behind the maze of grocery pallets.

Andy had approached the baler with a handful of cardboard and saw it was switched off. Despite Michael's screams, he switched it back on. All Andy could hear was Ed, singing about a castle on a hill.

I was still in the office. Waiting for the night crew manager, who would never come because the tannoy system had been on the blink again.

Oblivious to the banging and shouting, Andy saw the bale light was flashing now. He didn't question it and pressed the button to complete the bale while Ed continued to play in his earbuds.

I had heard it from the night crew manager's office... The baler machine was back on...

Then the guttural noises and the strain of metal.

Michael was killed at 6:00 a.m.

I snapped back to reality and the present day. The baler machine stood in front of me. It was empty.

No cardboard...

No Michael... And no Andy.

I rubbed my watery eyes and headed to my office. I can't take this anymore.

Please just stop.

I was halfway across the warehouse when I could hear it already. Guitar music...

A lonely haunting sound, coming from my office. I walked to the door and pushed it open.

"Hi, boss." Michael said, with Andy sitting beside him, earbuds in, strumming away on his guitar.

I wanted to scream at Michael, but I knew he was not real.

"So, boss. How are you finding your new job?"

I stood opposite Michael while Andy kept strumming on his guitar.

"Not quite what you expected, boss?"

I rubbed my eyes. Michael was still there and that flaming guitar music.

"What made you do it, boss? Was it this job? I mean, I was always going to be favourite to get it. Why would they give it to someone like you?"

Water welled in my eyes. I could no longer keep going. I wasn't going to make Christmas Day. Like a plastic ruler bent in two, I could feel myself about to snap.

"Or were you jealous of me and Hayley, boss? She is way too nice a person for you, by the way."

Snap.

I picked up a mug and hurled it at Michael. It went straight through him and smashed off the far wall, showering the room with pieces.

The guitar music kept playing.

"Leave me alone," I shouted. "It was an accident. I just wanted to scare you and I needed this job. I never meant for you to die." I thudded my head with the palm of my hand. This is not real. I'm talking to the dead.

"So, it wasn't just me and Hayley then, boss? I mean don't get me wrong, Hayley is nice and someone I liked as a friend, but she is not just my type. I'm more into the Ed Sheerans of this world, boss. Isn't that right, Andy?"

Andy just kept playing.

I stood there, shoulders heaving up and down with emotion. "Just leave me alone," I said, between the gasps in my breath. "I have had enough of this. It was an accident."

"An accident, boss? Mmm... that's borderline. But what isn't borderline is letting Andy here take all the blame for the *accident*. You had the brass neck to say you weren't even in the warehouse. When you realised what happened, you sneaked back out onto the shop floor and like the coward you are, you let someone else take the blame... Andy."

"I didn't mean for Andy..." I said.

"Look at Andy, boss."

Andy just kept playing.

"It destroyed him knowing he had pressed that button and killed me. The torment he suffered before he took his own life. I'm surprised he lasted two weeks before he wandered up to the electric room with the baler rope."

I slumped into my chair.

"I'm sorry," I sobbed. "But I can't go on. All this haunting me. I just want to do my job, get on with my life. I can't..."

"Well, do the right thing for once, boss. Tell Sue and Hayley the truth. They deserve to know and then we will leave you alone."

"I... I can't."

"If you want peace, you will," Michael said.

He then nodded towards Andy who stopped playing. "It's time for us to go, Andy."

Andy got up and held Michael's hand and then they were gone.

I slumped forward onto the desk, cutting myself on broken bits of the mug.

I had no way out...

Either own up and have no job, no Hayley, and be sent to prison on manslaughter charges...

Or continue this never-ending downward spiral of torment.

I looked up. It was the baler rope on the office shelf that caught my eye and the electrician who found me on Christmas

Eve.

Hanging in the electric room, at 6 o'clock in the morning.

The White Giant Cometh
Stephen Wade

Silence. Total and utter. The heavy snowfall had shrouded everything in white. Every tree, bush, and hedgerow, with resignation, supported new foliage of fallen snow.

No neighing or nickering of a horse could be heard. And neither did the lowing of a cow nor the braying of a donkey roll across the whitened fields. All domestic livestock had been stabled or safely locked away in barns and outhouses. The sheep too, the hardiest of all farm animals, Big Joe Kinsella had brought down from higher ground before the forecasted storm hit. Some of the farm animals, like the two miniature ponies and one of twin lambs that had been rejected by the ewe, Kinsella brought into the Christmas decoration festooned living room.

In the large kitchen, he constructed a pen for the lamb, and cordoned off part of the adjoining storeroom as a stable for the ponies.

Christmas week. Kinsella had time to get on with decorating. While his wife, Maura, was busy baking cakes for the Christmas fair.

Engrossed in their respective activities, the couple sang along from time to time to seasonal songs playing on the radio. But when the dulcet tones of Bowie and Bing came on duetting about the little drummer boy, they quickly turned the dial on the radio to another station. The same too at the intro to Johnny Mathis's sincere delivery of 'When a Child is Born'.

The loss of their only child to an undiagnosed, rare illness when the little boy had grown into a smiling and engaging personality was something the ageing couple never spoke about. The little boy who so cruelly left them forever on the morning when other children were opening gifts brought by Santa. The day when their little boy turned three.

From where he kept it in the main barn, Big Joe Kinsella brought in the old wicker basket which had served as their infant child's crib for the first few weeks of his short life.

With a few handfuls of straw in the crib, Kinsella put the lamb into it. There, the little creature bleated its high-pitched bleat a few times, before lying down and closing its eyes to sleep. The two miniature ponies, seemingly curious, put their heads over the half door Kinsella had constructed between the open storeroom door and the kitchen. One of them whinnied. The other hoofed the concrete floor, steam snorting from its nostrils.

Outside, the muted land, like a sleeping giant, was awakening. From the White Giant's yawning mouth came a howling wind. Its hoary breath releasing swirling showers of snowflakes that painted afresh the fields, hills and all their features. Into a seated position pushed the giant. And then, with a shake of his great white mane, he worked himself to his feet. And, as though he were trying to gain entry into Kinsella's home, he tapped the kitchen window with his icy fingertips, the crackle and whip of his cadaverous cloak flapping about his shoulders.

Startled, the miniature ponies reared up and neighed. The lamb bleated but remained in its crib.

Not until the Giant had exhausted himself did the ponies begin to settle down. Kinsella, who had stayed with them throughout the storm, ran his rough palms over their polls, necks, and forelocks. And exhaling from his mouth into their nostrils, he spoke softly.

"All right, lads," he said. "Let's get you both inside to the warmth. It's like a freezer in here."

Kinsella felt the White Giant's unforgiving Arctic breath breathe upon him when he opened the kitchen door to the elements. The freshly fallen snow made it easy to make it across the yard to the outhouses. From the larger barn he took an unused wooden trough and carried it back to the kitchen.

Before turning in that night, Kinsella gave the ponies some carrots and apples as treats.

Maura bottle-fed the lamb and sang to it a nursery rhyme about little stars twinkling. Although the song brought to Kinsella's mind the piping voice and memories of the child he never wanted to forget but was likewise too painful to remember, he hummed along to his wife's singing. The first time in over two decades either of them had allowed themselves to sing a song filled with such evocative words and images.

Maura wept herself to sleep that night. Kinsella hardly slept. And, when he did grab snatches of sleep, he dreamt. His dreams crowded with the wide-eyed, innocent face of a baby boy staring at a musical carousel box and listening to the tinkling song about stars looking down from a bright sky, and a child king asleep in hay.

Christmas Eve came. The White Giant by now a permanent guest on the farm. His presence everywhere. From the land and the sky every colour replaced by black and white and shadows of blue. Listless were the birds perched in the trees, as they awaited his departure. Their singing voices silenced - all except the song of the robin.

Perched on the rim of an old tin bucket just inside the door of the milking parlour, the robin's liquid warbling filled the small interior. Kinsella wrapped his thumb and forefinger about a cow's teat and squeezed down. The sound of the squirts of milk hitting the steel of the bucket wove into the robin's melodic singing, producing a wild, untamed chord.

At twelve midnight, the bells from the distant chapel tolled, ringing in the sacred day. Kinsella went to the bedroom window and opened it so he and his wife could hear clearer the pealing of the bells. The ringing entered the room and he felt it in his chest as though it were his own heartbeat. But something else took his attention. He removed his spectacles and wiped away the condensation with his handkerchief. He put them back on and squinted into the white night.

On the upper hills, silhouetted against the backdrop of the moon, there were some figures. What appeared to be two people, one walking and the other atop a horse. He called Maura, his wife, to his side. Together they watched as the figures made their way towards the house.

When the strangers were close enough to make out as a man on foot and a woman on the horse, the man waved up at them: a wave of reassurance. Kinsella and his wife waved back.

"Be careful," Maura said to Kinsella as he left their bedroom to go downstairs to meet their unexpected guests. A little less steady on her feet, Maura followed him at a slower pace.

Kinsella stepped out the front door, careful not to slip on the compacted and frozen snow. About to speak to the stranger, he stopped. He felt that something was not exactly wrong, but neither was it right. His body told him. The man's face, illuminated by the whiteness of the snow under moonlight, Kinsella felt he had seen before. In dreams maybe. His body shape too, and his carriage. The way he stood with his feet apart, his head tilted to one side.

The man spoke to Kinsella a few paces from the front door.

"Sorry for troubling you, Boss," he said. "But we're in a spot of bother." He gave a short laugh. But it was a laugh of apology and mild desperation.

"Come on in," Kinsella said, as he stepped out the door and took the horse by the halter, while the man helped the woman from its back. Only then did Kinsella realise that the man, this stranger, seemed no stranger at all. Looking at him, his movements, the way he squinted as though he normally wore glasses, and the way he swallowed before opening his mouth. And the woman, too, when she came out from under her headscarf and glanced at him through almond-shaped eyes. A familiar dimple in her left cheek. Kinsella might have been watching a home movie of himself and Maura made some decades back.

The man then helped the heavily pregnant woman into Kinsella's house, where Maura tended to her in the sitting room, while the two men brought the horse to the stables.

Kinsella watched the stranger remove the horse's saddle and halter. The way he whispered to the animal and stroked its flanks, every eye crease and shift of the stranger's feet he knew. For they were his own movements. And when this young man forked some hay before the horse, Kinsella felt the heft of the fork in his own hands.

Without conversing, the younger man then tended to Kinsella's other horses. The animals behaved as though they knew him. Seated on a bale of straw, Kinsella stayed put when the man left the stables to feed and water the rest of the livestock in the other outhouses. This too wasn't communicated between the two men. But Kinsella sensed what he was up to.

Heated and sleepy as he might have been at the end of a hard day's toiling, Kinsella closed his eyes. But when he reopened them, he was in the barn before the indoor sheep pen. Their troughs freshly filled with ewe nuts and grass nuts. And they had been watered.

In his hands Kinsella clutched an empty plastic feed bag.

Around the barn he scanned for the stranger. But no sign was there of him. Had not all the livestock been fed and watered,

Kinsella might have questioned the younger man's existence. Or his own sanity.

Heading back to the farmhouse, Kinsella heard lilting voices joined in song. The words of the song hailing the birth of a child on a calm night. A silent and holy night. But one voice soared above the others. A voice as pure as fresh snowfall cast upon the earth by the White Giant. A voice he knew and cherished in memory. But it couldn't be. Could it?

Through the front door and into the kitchen Kinsella strode. Unaware yet that he was walking without a limp. He stopped in the doorway of the kitchen. There before him, lying on a blanket in the straw on the floor and propped up by cushions was his wife, Maura. Maura as she had been when she bore their baby boy. And cradled in her arms that beautiful child as he was on the day of his birth.

Gathered round her were three men who turned to greet him. They pushed to their feet from the kneeling positions in which they were in.

"Dad," Kinsella said, as his deceased father, younger than Kinsella, came to him and embraced him.

The other two men laughed good-naturedly and applauded. Kinsella smiled at them over his father's shoulder. The older man he recognised as his uncle, his father's brother, who had long ago left for a life in the eastern part of the world. The younger man the brother Kinsella had neither seen nor spoken to for decades since they had fallen out over ownership of the land Kinsella farmed.

Led by his father, Kinsella pushed past the two ponies nuzzling at his hands. He kissed his wife tenderly and stroked their infant child's cheek. Maura jokingly admonished the three men for their thoughtful offerings of a gift card, baby oil and baby cologne.

The following day they awoke to the drip-drip of the icicles on the eaves of the roof beginning to melt. The first signs that the White Giant was getting ready to steal away. The blackbird and the wren followed the robin's lead. And were soon joined by the chaffinch, the pheasant, the warblers, the thrush, the dunnock, and the goldfinch. An avian orchestra to celebrate the rebirth of their baby child.

And while Kinsella took in the appetising aroma of the breakfast he was preparing for himself and Maura, the sizzle of rashers and the crackling of eggs frying on the pan was accompanied by a new sound. The most wondrous of family-life sounds. The sound of a newborn baby's cry.

Not For Human Consumption
Simon Horrocks

It was the first day of December – a Wednesday. With the start of a new month came a change in the shift. So, for the duration of December, I'd be on earlies. That meant the opening up of the indoor market was mine and Nathan's responsibility.

My boots left deep impressions as I trudged through a thick blanket of snow that had fallen overnight. It was still dark, bitterly cold and there wasn't a soul around. I passed rows of empty outdoor market stalls, it would be another two hours before the outdoor traders arrived, if any of them were brave enough. I clasped my council issue fleece tighter around my neck. I glanced up at the clock on the market clock tower - I could just about see the position of the spindly hands; they read ten-to-six. I knew there'd be a handful of traders outside the main door waiting for me, stamping their feet and grumbling for me to get a move on. It wasn't worth the bother telling them that my shift didn't start for another ten minutes.

I hoped Nathan would have already opened up and had the kettle on. Good old Nathan. Nathan had worked at the market since he had left school. Now in his late twenties, he was a big lad - strong too. But he was the butt of the other lads' jokes and wind-ups. Russ and Geoff were the main culprits - they'd hide his rucksack or the sandwiches his mum had made for him, or fasten his locker door with cable ties. Although Nathan didn't see it that way, most of it was harmless, but other times it was darker and nastier. Once, I thought of bringing it to the attention of the market officers, but no doubt word would have gotten out that I'd grassed and - if there was one thing I had learned in the few months since I'd started the job - it was that you didn't snitch on your workmates. So, I kept my mouth shut.

As I didn't tease him like the others did, he seemed to trust me. He'd grumble to me about the others; who'd done this to who or hadn't done that. When he spoke it was a low, barely audible mumble and, when I had first started, I had to ask him to repeat himself a number of times to the point of being rude. Occasionally, we'd be sat in the brew room and he'd be thumbing through his phone. He'd lean his large frame across the table and pass his phone to me.

"What does that say?" he'd mumble, and I'd have to read out some inane post on Facebook, much to the amusement of the others. I'd hand him back his phone and he'd just grunt. A lifetime of having to ask people to read things out for him had eroded his will to show gratitude.

I had reached the main door. Surprisingly, there was no-one waiting for me, and I breathed a sigh of relief. It was odd there were no traders, but at that moment all I cared about was escaping the cold, so I didn't give it a second thought.

After switching off the alarm I made my way to the basement. The indoor market was a huge Victorian building that dated back to the 1840s. For 150 years the market had been the bustling hub of the town. But the growth of the supermarket and the boom in online shopping over recent years had whittled down the number of stalls. Greengrocers, butchers, cafés, mobile phone repair shops, haberdasheries and babies clothing stalls were some of the traders that had survived, frequented by a legion of loyal customers, a lot of them elderly, who saw a trip to the market as day out. Still, there was enough work to keep all us porters busy: taking away the traders' cardboard, attending to spillages, clearing the rubbish, and generally keeping the place clean.

Down in the basement it was just as cold as it was outside. I switched the lights on in the brew room, grabbed a walkie-talkie from the charging docks and filled up the kettle. There was no sign of Nathan. The sink was full of dirty dishes bathing in filthy water. The kitchen worktop was a patchwork quilt of spillages, and the bin was overflowing. On my first day at work the market officer had showed me around.

"You can tell this is the cleaners' room by how dirty it is," he had joked.

I tried to contact Nathan on my walkie-talkie. It was mandatory to carry one at all times when on shift (mainly so the market officers could bark their orders at us wherever we were).

"Simon to Nathan? Nathan, are you here?"

Static crackled from the radio as I waited

for a reply. When none came, I tried again and then again. With a sigh, I gave up. I checked the clock on the wall: five-past-six. Nathan was late. We'd been told in team meetings that if your partner didn't show up on time for opening, you had to report it. It was a regular occurrence, more often due to a hangover and it was always the same culprits. But, as ever, you kept quiet about it.

Feeling a little angry with Nathan that he was late, I gave up making the tea and made my way from the brew room to make a start on my own. I crossed the large stock room where the dry goods traders kept their surplus stock and out into the main corridor.

At the far end of the corridor was the goods lift and opposite that was the baling room.

The market basement was a rabbit warren of dark corridors and forbidden rooms which were strictly out of bounds. Whenever I was down there alone, I would be constantly checking my back. It was just that kind of place. 'DANGER. NO UNAUTHORIZED PERSONNEL' read the signs on the doors in large, bold letters. Some of the rooms hadn't been entered for years. Who knew what was lurking in them?

Something maybe lay festering. Living. Breathing. Waiting. It was no coincidence that the 'danger' was unexplained and instead left to your own imagination.

The corridor was eerily quiet. Usually at that time you would hear the rumble of pallet trucks from above as the traders set out their stalls. I sensed a presence.

"Nathan? Are you there?" I called out - there was no reply.

As I crept slowly down the corridor, I noticed all the doors were open with their lights on. Feeling a little uneasy, I quickly checked each room for a sign of life, the word 'DANGER' flashing before me, I was in and out of each room in an instant, pulling the door shut behind me.

I had reached the baling room. I called Nathan again, this time with a hint of anger to my tone but, yet again, there was no response. The baling room was a vast space where all the bins, rubbish and cardboard collected from the indoor and outdoor market were kept. The silent army of cardboard cages, cardboard bales and bins threw long shadows across the concrete floor. There was a bright yellow button flashing on one of the balers indicating that the bale was ready. Why hadn't the evening shift dealt with it? Lazy bastards.

It was even colder in the baling room than it was in the corridor and the only sound was from the low hum of the insect-o-cuter on the wall with its fluorescent cyan tubes. I soon realised what was causing the unusual chill. In the corner of the room was the huge walk-in fridge where the offal bins were stored and its door had been left ajar. I decided to check inside the fridge, just in case Nathan was working in there. I ducked my head inside.

The light was blinding and the freezing cold stung my cheeks and nose. There was no sign of Nathan. Four red offal bins formed a line. There should have been five; two for the butchers, one for the fishmongers and two spare - so one was missing. Each bin had 'NOT FOR HUMAN CONSUMPTION' emblazoned on the front. I'd never dared to lift the lid of one of those bins and peer inside - what I'd likely see would put me off eating meat for ever. When they were full, they weighed a tonne, and I could only push one at a time. Nathan could shift two at once without breaking a sweat.

After bolting the heavy fridge door, I looked around for the missing bin. To my right were neat rows of the brown wheelie bins which were used by the greengrocers and the florists, and alongside them were the huge eleven-hundred bins we threw all the general waste in. The rest of the baling room was taken up by the cardboard bales; at least fifty of them were sat on wooden pallets. I couldn't see the missing offal bin. Looking around at the bales and bins in their neat regiments, I felt as if they were watching me. My eyes flitted from one corner of the vast room to the other. Was someone hiding in here, lurking in one of the eleven-hundreds or ducking behind the bales of cardboard? The button on the baler was still flashing yellow. I heard a buzz of electricity that made me jump - the insect-o-cuter had claimed another victim.

I checked the time on my phone: 06:18. I wondered if Nathan had called one of the market officers to say he'd be late or was off sick. I had no way of knowing, there was no reception in the basement so, if I had a text or a voice message from anyone, I couldn't access it. The eleven-hundreds needed to be put outside for refuse to collect. It was a two-man job; one to load the goods lift with the bins in the basement and one to take them out of the lift upstairs and put them outside. I cursed at the thought of doing all that alone, but it had to be done. Nathan would have to owe me one.

I dragged an eleven-hundred out to the goods lift. By the side of the lift was another sign, 'GOODS LIFT ONLY. NO PERSONNEL.'

Before I opened the steel concertina door, I decided to try to contact Nathan again on his walkie-talkie. Even though he wasn't the kind of bloke for practical jokes, if he was hiding in the goods lift waiting to spring out on me, his walkie-talkie would give him away. I pressed the button to speak.

"Simon to Nathan?" I stood still and stared at the walkie-talkie, willing the red light to come on, indicating that someone was about to communicate. I waited and waited. After a while, I gave a deep sigh. "For God's sake Nathan," I muttered under my breath. I waited some more and then tried again out of sheer desperation. "Nathan, where are you? I need help with these eleven-hundreds..." I glanced up the corridor... all the doors were wide open again and their lights on.

I wasn't alone. I felt a shiver slip down my spine.

"Come on, Nathan,' I shouted in a quivering tone, 'we haven't got time for this..."

Once again there was only stubborn silence. I stared at each door in turn... who or what was lurking behind them?

"Is there someone there? Is that you, Geoff? Russ...? Danny...? Come on, lads, stop arsing about..."

I stood there for what seemed like an eternity waiting for someone to assure me that I wasn't going mad. I tried my walkie-talkie again, keeping my eyes on the corridor.

"Market office... come in... market office... come... is anyone there at all...?" Predictably, there was no red light and no reply. I checked the time again, 06:26. The refuse collection turned up at a quarter-to-seven, if I didn't get all the eleven-hundreds out in time I'd miss them, then I'd be in the shit. I yanked open the lift doors, there was a screech of steel against steel like fingernails down a chalkboard. As the door opened, I was greeted by a pitch-black cavern and a nauseating smell. I held my hand to my mouth and coughed - even after several weeks at the market I'd still not got used to that sickening odour and it seemed to be worse than ever. There was a large, red object in one dark corner of the lift. It was the missing offal bin.

"For God's sake!!" I bellowed. I stomped into the lift and grabbed the handle of the bin, when suddenly the lift doors screeched shut behind me with a clatter.

I spun around. "What the...?"

There was no door handle on the inside of the lift so I tried to grip what I could of the door with my fingers. With gritted teeth I pulled as hard as I could until the tips of my fingers turned white and throbbed with pain. When I couldn't take the pain any longer, I kicked the lift door as hard as I could.

"Come on, I've had enough of this shit now! Let me out!"

I peered through the small window in the lift door, expecting to see a couple of the lads, doubled over in uncontrollable laughter at their prank, but no-one was there. Perhaps they were crouched below the lift window out of sight - giggling like schoolgirls. But would any of them really venture out to work at this time of the morning in deep snow, just to play a joke on me? It seemed unlikely. I jabbed at the lift's emergency button. It glowed red and the alarm screeched. The alarm would be sounding in the empty market office; they'd be no one there yet for at least another hour.

I tried my walkie-talkie again... and again. I threw it to the floor in frustration and it hit the corrugated metal floor with a bang. Its battery flew out and disappeared into the darkness. *Brilliant*, I thought indignantly, *that's just what I need.* I peered through the window again, trying to see up the corridor.

It was still desolate and all the doors were shut.

A whimper fell from my mouth and my legs gave way as I collapsed to the floor.

I was on my hands and knees. I could feel the cold of the metal against my palms. Down on the floor the lift's smell was even more revolting and I had to try hard to stop myself from vomiting. I decided to see if I could find the battery and I fumbled around for it like a blind man.

Just then the lights from the window went out and I was shrouded in a cloak of darkness. For a few seconds I froze. Then, I slowly hauled myself up off the floor. I couldn't see the rest of my body, which was disorientating. I took a couple of steps backward and leaned against the side of the lift. I took a deep breath, trying to calm myself and think straight. From above my head, I heard a whirring sound and the lift shunted into life. I felt the lift floor shift beneath my feet and I lost my balance, then quickly regained it. The lift wobbled to-and-fro as it headed upwards until it came to a stop.

There were only two levels for the goods lift; basement and main market hall. I was still surrounded by darkness and couldn't see a thing out of the lift window. It was still at least another hour before the sun rose and light would come pouring through the skylights in the market hall. Suddenly, I remembered that my phone had a torch. I reached into my pocket and swiped on the torch, which threw a circle of light against the door. I shone it at the window. The stalls were all empty and there wasn't a soul around. I tried every angle, craning my neck to see up and down the walkways between stalls. I stabbed at the alarm again and again, the shrill sound screaming my panic around the abandoned hall. Out of sheer frustration, I kicked the lift door over and over until my toes went numb. I slid down the side of the lift and sat down, my head in my hands.

So, there I was: imprisoned in a steel tomb with only an offal bin for company, waiting to be rescued. I was bound to have missed the collection for the eleven-hundreds, that meant the bins would be overflowing all day with two days' worth of waste. I'd be summoned to the office for a lecture; my heart sank at the thought. When this was over, I'd be the butt of the lads' jokes. I'd just have to take it in good humour, I thought. Laugh it off until they got bored and turned their attention back to Nathan.

A sudden sound interrupted my thoughts.

A scratching.

Then it stopped.

I held my breath to listen.

There was more scratching.

The sound was definitely inside the lift with me. I grabbed my phone and aimed the torch light from where I thought the sound was coming from. I couldn't see anything but grubby steel walls.

There it was again.

I pointed the torch in another direction but there was nothing there. What the hell was it? Rats?

More scratching.

I checked all around the lift, when there was only one place left to check I felt an immovable object in my mouth. I swallowed hard. Not wanting to, but needing to, I slowly let the light land on the offal bin. I realised my head was shaking. I recoiled in disgust. The circle of light quivered as my hand shook. The scratching continued. I cowered in the corner, unable to take the light away from the bin.

Then there came a grunt, then a snort. I yelped and cowered tighter in the corner. The bin rocked. More scratching and then snorting. The lid lifted slightly and a blast of repugnant air shot out. The bin continued to rock, I reached out my hand, unable to draw it back. I moved closer to the bin, my hand trembling.

A voice inside my head shouted, "Don't do it! Don't do it!" I was within a few inches of the bin when the lid lifted again. There was an almighty snort, I felt warm air on my fingertips and my arm was showered with spray and the stench made my eyes water.

I had my fingers under the lid.

"No! No! No! No!"

The bin rocked from side-to-side almost toppling over.

I yanked back my arm, and spun away from the bin.

There was a face at the window.

I screamed.

It was Nathan.

Relief washed over me, then I felt a sting of embarrassment.

Nathan hauled open the lift door and light flooded in.

"What you doin'? Been trying to get you on the radio..." he mumbled, a puzzled look on his face.

From behind him I heard the chatter of the traders and the rumble of pallet trucks.

Over at the bakery they were filling the shelves with freshly baked bread and the greengrocer was laying out his apples into orderly rows, whistling as he worked.

A whiff of bacon spitting on the grill wafted my way from one of the market cafés. Normally - at that time of the morning - that would have made my mouth water and my stomach rumble.

But that moment was about as far away from normal as you could get and, from that day to this, I've been vegetarian.

The Last Bus
Pamela Morrison

It was a foul November night. Rain lashed the windscreen, and the bus swayed under the force of the gale. Charlie hated the late shift, but he was on the final run now. It was late night shopping on a Thursday, and he'd had a full load of passengers when he left town. They'd bundled onto the bus, laden with shopping bags and squabbling kids. An aroma of wet wool and wet hair had percolated through the vehicle, and the windows had steamed up with condensation.

When all the passengers had been dropped off, Charlie started to wend his way back to the depot along winding country lanes. He passed scattered cottages where lit windows showed family tableaux: tables set for tea, the comforting glow of a log fire, children playing on a fireside rug. It made Charlie long for the comfort of his own home. He'd only been married for a few months, and he relished every moment of his new life with Marianne.

The final leg of his journey was up Emmett's Hill, before descending to cross the bridge and follow the river valley back to town. The rain had stopped now, but the wind was fierce. Wet leaves and twigs hurled against the windscreen. Ahead, the road twisted up the steep slope of Emmett's Hill, disappearing like a silver serpent into the dark tunnel of trees.

Charlie anticipated a straight run home with no more fares. But wait a moment, wasn't that a figure standing in the shadows halfway up the hill? He peered into the constantly moving mass of shadows. The bus was 'request only' at this stage of the journey, but he didn't want to leave anyone stranded, especially not on a night like this.

A tall, thin figure in a black coat was standing at the edge of the woods. Charlie slowed and looked more closely. The man made no signal for the bus to stop. He was turned away from the road and gazing into the wood. *Probably a dog walker*, decided

Charlie, and drove on.

He glanced in his mirror a short time later and saw the figure battling up the hill into the wind. *Damn, thought Charlie, I can't leave him out there on a night like this.*

There was no sign of a dog; maybe he did want the bus after all.

Charlie pulled in to the side of the road and waited as the figure drew closer. It was moving at a painfully slow speed and seemed to flicker in the shifting shadows of the swaying trees. Charlie considered reversing down the road to meet him, but the bus was already in the dark tunnel of trees, and it seemed too dangerous to back up. Sighing, Charlie opened the power-assisted passenger door, and waited. He drowsily leaned his head against the steamy window and dreamt of home and Marianne. He visualised walking through the front door to the tantalising aroma of a home-cooked meal. Marianne was cooking his favourite tonight: shepherd's pie.

The wail of a police car siren roused him. Glancing in the mirror, he could see the flashing blue light coming up the hill. He switched on his hazard warning lights. It was pitch black here in the woods and he didn't want to cause an accident. A few moments later, a police car hurtled past, followed by another. The banshee scream of their sirens set Charlie's nerves on edge. He was anxious to get going now. He glanced at his watch. Ten minutes had passed. Ten minutes! Had he fallen asleep? He looked in the mirror, and felt an icy shiver run down his spine as he surveyed the road behind him.

The man in the long dark coat was still there. He hadn't moved any further forward – yet he was still walking. It seemed to Charlie that he was hovering above the road. Charlie blinked and rubbed his eyes. No, there was no mistake; the man was hovering about a foot above the road. His legs were in motion, but his head was held to one side at a strange angle. I'm getting out of here, thought Charlie. He fired the ignition and closed the passenger doors. Shakily, he edged out into the road.

The bus gathered speed. Charlie changed up a gear and leaned forward, willing the bus to go faster. He was ten minutes behind schedule now, and that was frowned upon by his colleagues. It affected the performance rating of the entire team and could mean a loss of bonus points. He pushed all thoughts of the roadside figure out of his mind and focused on the road ahead. Soon, he would reach the brow of the hill and could hurtle down the other side towards the river crossing and home.

Suddenly, an eerie blue glow appeared rushing down the hill towards him. Unnerved by his earlier experience, Charlie slammed his foot on the brakes. Too late, he realised that it was only a returning police car. The steering wheel spun beneath his hands as the bus went into a skid. The back of the vehicle slewed across the road. Images of dark trees flickered across the windscreen. Charlie braced himself for the impact, the awful crunch of soft flesh against glass and steel. He thought of Marianne and screamed out her name. Then, almost in slow motion, the bus began to slide in the opposite direction. It ploughed through the roadside ferns and bracken before stopping, half on and half off the road.

Charlie clutched the steering wheel and stared through the windscreen at the blue flickering image of a human face. It took a moment before he realised that it was a policeman whose vehicle was now parked on the opposite side of the road, blue lights still flashing. Charlie wound down his window and took great gulps of air. He could smell the pungent aroma of damp leaves and moss, and hear the distant screech of an owl. His senses were heightened by the shock.

"Are you alright?" asked the policeman. "That was quite some skid. I've never seen anything like it. You were heading straight for the trees. I thought you were a goner, but the bus righted itself at the last moment."

"I'm all right. I need to get going now. I'm already behind schedule."

"Well, you can't go this way," said the policeman. "The road is closed up ahead."

"Has there been an accident?" said Charlie.

"The bridge has collapsed. The force of the storm water was too much for it. The whole thing has collapsed into the river. It's lucky you weren't ten minutes earlier. You would have gone with it."

Charlie stared at him, open-mouthed.

"Are you sure you're all right, sir?" asked the policeman. "You look as if you've seen a ghost."

"D-d-did you see him?" stuttered Charlie. "I mean, earlier, when you passed me? Did you see a man at the side of the road, sort of hovering...?"

"There was no-one around when I drove up. Maybe you saw Emmett's ghost." The policeman gave a nervous chuckle to show that he didn't believe in such rubbish.

"Who's Emmett?" asked Charlie.

"The bloke who owned these woods. Way back, it must have been twenty years ago, he was a young newly-wed and he bought a house back in the village there. Well, one night, so the story goes, he'd had a few too many jars in the pub. When he got home, his wife remonstrated with him and, in his drunken state, he lashed out at her. His wife was distraught. Said she didn't want to be married to a violent bully and she packed her bags and left. It was a wild night like this one and, as she drove down the hill, she lost control. The car skidded and went through the hedge into the river. Emmett was distraught. He vowed he would never touch a drop of alcohol again."

"And did he?"

"He didn't really have the chance. He hanged himself next day. His body was found swinging from an oak tree just back there. Are you all right, sir? You really do look as if you've seen a ghost."

The White Widow
Simon Horrocks
2nd Place

From: gareth.armstrong95@gmail.com
To: kimberley.young94@gmail.com
Date: 22 October, 16:04

Hey,

How's the conference going?

Well, I've arrived safe and sound; the journey took me just under two hours, which isn't too bad in that old banger of mine! The guest house is very comfortable (if a little bit dated) and it's run by Eve and

Tom, who've made me feel really welcome. They're originally from the North East and they moved here about ten years ago.

After I had unpacked, I went out exploring the town. The whole place has been decked out for Halloween; skeletons, cobwebs, witches and pumpkins everywhere! The town's not as popular as other parts of the Lake District such as Windermere or Keswick, but no less picturesque. I've taken quite a few pictures: the bustling market in the town square, the medieval church and the nearby lake.

Okay, confession time; I've had a bit of a disaster... I've broken my phone (doh!!). It fell out of the pocket of my shorts down by the lakeside and hit a rock. There's now a crack across the screen like a bolt of lightning and when I tried to turn the thing on, I was greeted with a blinking question mark.

So, that's the reason I'm emailing you and not texting or phoning.

Currently, I'm processing today's photos on my laptop, but it's taking ages (I really need a new computer, but I guess that's out of the question with our wedding and the new house to pay for).

Tom's told me about an abandoned slate mine that he said I should investigate, which sounds interesting, so I'm planning on exploring that tomorrow afternoon. In the morning I'm climbing Lam Tor. It's the highest of fells that surround the town and Tom has very kindly shown me the best route to the summit. I'm going to be up before sunrise and hopefully I'll get some awesome pics.

Anyway, I'm going to spend a couple of hours adjusting today's photos in Lightroom and Photoshop, then I'm off into town to find a chippy.

Speak soon,
G x

From: gareth.armstrong95@gmail.com
To: kimberley.young94@gmail.com
Date: 23 October, 10:14

Hey,

Hope your day's going well?

So far, I've had a bit of an odd morning. Here's what happened...

It was still dark when I left the guest house and there was a sharp chill in the air - a stark reminder of the coming winter. I wanted to be up at the top as the sun came, the 'Golden Hour' as we photographers call it. I strapped a miner's light over my woolly hat and carried a torch, but I needed to be careful in the limited light, so I was going to take my time with the ascent. Lam Tor's summit is over two thousand feet above sea level, and it would take me about ninety minutes to reach it.

It was a twenty-minute walk to the foot of the mountain, which sits on the outskirts of the sleeping town. Once I was there, shrouded in darkness, I shone my torch at the wooden fingerpost. It read, 'LAM TOR SUMMIT. 3 MILES.' For a second, I wondered whether I should turn back – it was hard enough making the attempt in full light, in darkness it was probably madness. But you know me, I like a challenge. So, I pointed the torch in the direction of the fingerpost and followed the circle of light into the unknown.

The first few hundred yards up the mountain path were fairly easy but then my calf muscles began to throb as the ascent grew steeper. My breathing became more laboured the higher I climbed, and a cold sweat slid down my spine. I hadn't realised how unfit I was until now. I had thought that the hours spent at the gym would prepare me for this, but how wrong I was. (Perhaps if I'd have spent more time on the treadmill instead of the sauna it may have helped.)

Alone in the dark the only sounds were my heavy breathing and the crunch of gravel underneath my boots. My heart was thumping madly in my chest, and I stopped to take a few long, deep breaths. My mouth was as dry as sawdust and I greedily gulped down a couple of bottles of water. I pushed on. A strong gust of wind tried to propel me back and, as the route got even steeper, I slipped on some wet pebbles and fell face down on the path, cutting the palm of my hand and grazing my knee in the process.

Every muscle in my legs protested under the strain but I was determined to make it to the top before the sun came up and soon enough, after a few more stops and slips, the sky faded from ultramarine to cobalt and the top of the mountain loomed just above me in silhouette.

The last bit of the climb was the hardest and I reached the top on all fours like a mountain lion. Relieved to have done it, I waited for my breathing to slow down. The wind had dropped to a whisper and my face was slick with salty sweat. The pain in my legs began to subside to a dull ache that was somehow satisfying. I took in lungfuls of sweet, clean air and suddenly my mood was elevated. The morning sun hovered just above the horizon – peeping through the gaps between the mountains. I grabbed my camera from my rucksack and reeled off some shots of the lake below with the majestic mountains in the background.

In the milky, early morning light, I surveyed the rest of the route. The mountain levelled off for about a quarter of a mile before a final, steep (but, thankfully, short) ascent to the summit. The path dipped and rolled all the way over the grassy terrain and, at a cairn, I paused and poured myself a steaming cup of coffee from a tartan flask which Eve had lent me. The views were breath-taking. I guessed I could see for twenty miles or so. The mountains crowded the skyline like a platoon of giants marching towards me. The valley below was a patchwork of fields with sheep scattered about them like confetti. Beyond the fields, the lake, like a shard of frozen ink. And, at the far side of the lake, the town, sprawling like a spillage of Lego bricks. I picked out the steeple of the medieval church I had visited yesterday, and was trying to locate my guest house when cloud rolled in from behind me, smothering me in white smoke. For a few minutes I sat waiting for the cloud to pass, drinking my coffee, and, as the last whisps disappeared, I put my flask back in my rucksack and continued on.

I whistled as I walked along, enjoying the scenery, when suddenly the light dimmed and the heavens opened. With a shadow above following me, the wind made sure that I was pelted with rain hard enough to sting my eyes. I bowed my head and followed the path as I had done with the climb. At one point it got so dark that I had to switch my torch back on. I glanced up to see how far away from the summit I was and that was when I saw, a few hundred yards or so ahead of me, a woman in a white dress.

I slowed down. I was confused. Shocked. She wasn't there before the rain came down, was she? Surely, I would have noticed if she was - she looked completely incongruous against the landscape and the backdrop of the graphite, wet sky. She stood at the mountain's edge, next to a formation of boulders, looking out. Just a few feet from where she was standing was a sheer drop and I felt a flutter of nerves in the pit of my stomach.

As I drew closer, I could see she was young - early twenties - and she was holding a small bouquet of brown, drooping flowers. Her hair was blonde, in tight, neat waves - the kind of style I'd seen in wartime movies. Her lips were cherry red, and her complexion was as pale as her dress. She had one limp hand by her side and her soggy bouquet in the other. I plucked up the courage to say something and I had to shout to be heard above the bellow of the wind.

"Hello, can I help you? Are you lost?"

She ignored me or didn't hear. I repeated myself, but she continued to stare out, lost in her thoughts. I crept slowly forwards, so as not to alarm her.

"Er... hello there... are you okay? Can I help you?"

She looked like a porcelain figurine teetering on the edge of a mantelpiece.

With just her dress to protect her from the elements she must have been freezing, or mad, or both. What on earth was she doing there? Was I witnessing a mental breakdown? Was she about to throw herself over the edge? Without my help - I thought - she may just do. Either that, or succumb to exposure.

I slid off my rucksack and unzipped my coat and held it out to her. My arm was extended towards her, the coat almost blowing out of my hand.

"Here," I said, "take this. You'll catch your death."

Very slowly, she turned her head towards me, like a clockwork ballerina in a music box. It may have been tears I saw rolling down her pale, sunken cheeks, but it could just as well have been the drizzle. She stared at me with her chestnut eyes in a way that was unsettling; they were glazed and hollow, as if they'd endured countless sleepless nights. After a few seconds, I looked away, unable to hold her stare. I dropped my coat and grabbed my rucksack, holding it out to her.

"Would you like some coffee? I have some here."

I knelt down and - with my hands shaking - I fumbled in my bag. I pulled out the flask and took off the cup. I placed the cup on the ground but the wind blew it over, so I held it between my knees. I unscrewed the lid of the flask, hands still trembling, and poured. I missed the cup and steaming coffee splashed onto my leg, causing me to yelp in pain. I carefully poured again, filling half a cup and then screwed the lid of the flask tight.

"There you are," I said, standing up, knees cracking like walnuts, but she'd vanished.

I gasped and dropped the cup. I darted for the precipice. The wind willed me to yield to its power and dive to my death, so I clung on to one of the boulders for dear life. I scanned the crag all the way to the bottom. There was a slate mine, hundreds of feet below, burrowed into the side of the mountain. It must have been the one Tom had mentioned. There was a rail track emanating from the mouth of the mine and an upturned hand cart, all in miniature. But no sign of the girl. I hauled myself back to safety.

I searched the boulders, checking every nook and cranny to see if that was where she was hiding. But I couldn't find her - she'd simply disappeared. I went back and picked up my coat and the cup, just saving it from being blown over the edge. Sitting down on a nearby rock, I poured myself a coffee. There was no trace of her. Not a single footprint. Not a solitary petal fallen from her bouquet. The image in my mind was the only evidence that she was ever there at all. I was alone again with just the rocks for company. I took in the view: the altitude and the vast, open, empty space were suddenly unnerving, almost threatening. A shiver slid down my back. I threw away the coffee, put the flask back in my rucksack and pushed on to the summit.

Gx

From: gareth.armstrong95@gmail.com
To: kimberley.young94@gmail.com
Date: 23 October, 11:59

Hey,

Quick update on the events of this morning. Back at the guest house, I checked the local news on the BBC website and there's been no accident on the fells or any reports of missing persons. I was thinking about reporting the girl, I googled Mountain Rescue and Cumbria police and there's a live chat on both websites and, whilst I mulled it over, I nipped out to get a sandwich.

Eve (the landlady) met me on the stairs carrying bedsheets up to one of the rooms.

"Oh, hello," she said,. "Hope you're enjoying you're stay with us so far?"

I told her about my trip up Lam Tor and mentioned the strange girl I'd seen.

"I'm a bit worried about her," I said. "I think she was having some sort of breakdown. Do you think I should report it to Mountain Rescue?"

She smiled, shaking her head.

"I don't think that'll be necessary, it was probably just a practical joke," she said.

I was a little bit taken aback.

"Sorry? I'm not sure I follow?"

"It'll be someone pretending to be a ghost."

"Really? What do you mean?"

"Our resident ghost...?"

I must have given her a blank look.

"Oh, so you haven't heard of her yet?" she said, laughing. "We have a local ghost. She's known as The White Widow around here. There's a ghost walk up the fells on a Thursday afternoon, it meets at the tourist information centre at... I forget now... 2 o'clock, I think. We have a leaflet about it in the breakfast room if you want to take one?"

"Oh, okay... but why..." In my head a million questions jostled to be asked first.

She laughed. "It's fine, don't worry about it,' she said, waving her hand dismissively. "Anyway, I must crack on." She went to go past me.

"Sorry, I hate to be rude," I said, "but how can you be sure it was a prank? It seemed pretty genuine to me?"

She sighed, wearing the kind of expression I imagine kids see when their parents explain that the tooth fairy doesn't exist.

"We have a drama college not far from here. They regularly perform a play about The White Widow. It was most likely one of the students messing around."

"Ahh, well, yeah, that seems... probable. Glad I didn't report it then. I'd have felt a right idiot," I said, not meeting her gaze, my cheeks burning crimson.

"Oh, don't worry about it," she laughed, attempting to go past me again.

I moved to my right, standing in her path.

"Is there a background story to it... the ghost I mean?"

"There is, you can read all about it in the leaflet. Let me get you one." She turned around and headed downstairs. I followed her.

"There you are," she said, handing me the leaflet and scampering back up the stairs in one movement.

Standing in the hallway, I read the backstory of The White Widow:

Sometime in the 1920s, a young couple lived in the town named Jake and Beryl. They'd been childhood sweethearts and were due to be married. In his spare time, Jake loved to walk on the surrounding fells. On the morning of their wedding, Jake set out for an early morning walk - probably to calm his nerves before the start of the big day. But, despite being an experienced hiker who knew the terrain well, he somehow fell to his death. Just as Beryl was heading for the altar, she was told of the accident and she died a year later of a broken heart. Ever since, she can be seen up on the fells, where Jake took his final walk.

I pocketed the leaflet and went back up to the first floor. Eve was busy pulling a sheet off a bed in one of the rooms, her back to me. I knocked on the door, she turned around.

"It's an interesting story," I said.

"Oh, it's just an urban myth, a bit of fun. Take it with a pinch of salt."

"But Jake and Beryl, were they real people?"

A fresh bedsheet billowed like a sail as she laid it on the bed.

"I'm not sure, actually. Tom will know."

"So, it may not be an urban myth then?"

"The supernatural bit is. Now, if you don't mind, I really need to get these beds made. Enjoy the rest of your afternoon. Take care. Bye."

What do you make of that?

Gx

From: gareth.armstrong95@gmail.com
To: kimberley.young94@gmail.com
Date: 23 October, 22:46

Hey,

Hope you're still up?

The plot thickens...

I was having a couple of pints in a pub not far from the guest house. It's one of those cosy places; low, oak-beamed ceilings, roaring fire, and a good selection of craft ales. I got talking to the landlord - turns out he's got a keen interest in photography too.

I asked him about The White Widow (I didn't mention that I might have seen her this morning, I didn't want him knowing that I'd been the gullible victim of some daft prank) and he confirmed the same story that the landlady had told me earlier.

What he also told me (that Eve hadn't) was that the legend goes that a sighting of The White Widow foretells of a death on the fells. But he dismissed it as a load of old mumbo-jumbo. He added that punters (usually giddy tourists) were always in his pub claiming that they'd seen her whilst out walking. It was a bit like spotting the Loch Ness Monster, he said.

Mumbo-jumbo it maybe but still interesting, eh?

Right, it's been quite an eventful day and I'm knackered, so I best say goodnight – I've got another early start tomorrow. Who knows what that'll bring? I'm heading up Craventrigg, it's not as high as Lam Tor but the terrain is more rugged. Tom has again very kindly pointed out the safest route to the summit. He thinks I'm bonkers attempting it before first light and no doubt you do too but, like I always say, if you want the best photos, you have the extra mile. LOL.

Gx

From: kimberley.young94@gmail.com
To: gareth.armstrong95@gmail.com
Date: 24 October, 15:15

Hey,

☹   Not heard from you yet today … is everything okay?

It's the last day of the conference tomorrow and I can't wait to get home. Some of it's been useful I suppose but the majority of it has been mind-bogglingly dull!

(I've been sneakily reading your emails on my phone during the boring bits – The White Widow is a fascinating story!)

Did you take any good photos today? When do I get to see them?

Write back soon…. that's an order!
Miss u
Kim xx

From: kimberley.young94@gmail.com
To: gareth.armstrong95@gmail.com
Date: 24 October, 20:32

Hey,

Are you ignoring me, mister? LOL

Just heading to the hotel resident's bar,
message me soon.

xx

From: tom@hatherleyguesthouse.com
To: kimberley.young94@gmail.com
Date: 30 October, 10:51

Dear Kimberley,

On behalf of my wife and I, allow us to offer you our most sincere condolences.

A tragedy on the fells is something of a rarity around these parts and hopefully the inquest will tell us more.

For the brief time we knew Gareth we found him to be a very charming and pleasant young man. We understand you were due to be married next year - we can only imagine your pain.

We've kept the room Gareth stayed in closed out of respect and we've put away his personal belongings. He has some clothes, a laptop computer, and a mobile phone. We'll keep them here until you're ready to pick them up - there's no rush.

With deepest sympathy,
Tom and Evelyn Egerton

www.crowvus.com

Praise for Ring-A-Ding Dead!

"A good fun read ..."

— NINJA LIBRARIAN

"Claire Logan spins a tale that keeps you interested and wanting to read more."

— SHERRY LEGAN

"All the characters are well developed, and the story is delightful."

— BARONESS BOOK TROVE

"Ring-A-Ding Dead! is two mysteries for the price of one."

— REBECCA M. DOUGLASS

"... my favorite thing about this novel is the characters, especially Hector and Pamela. My second favorite is that the action is fast-paced, so you have have to be on your toes at times when trying to figure out the killer yourself."

— MELISSA WILLIAMS

"I recommend this book to cozy mystery readers that enjoy the look and feel and flavor of Prohibition Chicago."

— KAREN SIDDALL

Praise for The Vanishing Valet!

"I enjoy the varied backgrounds of the characters in this novel and am very happy that Mrs. Jackson more or less takes the lead investigating role at times in this series."

— MORELL

"This charming mystery series reminds me of Nick and Nora Charles."

— VIRGINIA

"Entertaining story"

— VESPER

"Even better than a locked-door mystery is a no-door mystery."

— HEATHER

"We are transported back to the opulence of the 1920's ..."

— INFOSLEUTH